THE TAINOS

THE TAINOS

The People Who Welcomed Columbus

FRANCINE JACOBS

with illustrations by Patrick Collins

G. P. PUTNAM'S SONS   NEW YORK

The author wishes to thank Samuel M. Wilson,
Assistant Professor of Anthropology, University of Texas at Austin,
for checking the manuscript of this book.

Text copyright © 1992 by Francine Jacobs
Illustrations copyright © 1992 by Patrick Collins
Map by Jeanyee Wong
All rights reserved. This book, or parts therof, may not be
reproduced in any form without permission in writing from the publisher.
G. P. Putnam's Sons, a division of The Putnam & Grosset Group,
200 Madison Avenue, New York, NY 10016.
Published simultaneously in Canada.
Printed in the United States of America.
Book design by Patrick Collins

Library of Congress Cataloging-in-Publication Data
Jacobs, Francine.   The Tainos: The people who welcomed Columbus
/Francine Jacobs.   p.   cm.
Includes bibliographical references (p. 87) and index.
Summary: Describes the history, culture, and mysterious fate of
the first native Americans to welcome Columbus in 1492.
1. Taino Indians—Juvenile literature.   [1. Taino Indians.
2. Indians of the West Indies.]   I. Title.
F1619.2.T3J34   1992   972.9'01—dc20   91-3215   CIP   AC
ISBN 0-399-22116-6

5   7   9   10   8   6

For Emily and Douglas Stott
and Denise and Jerry Brown,
with affection

Contents

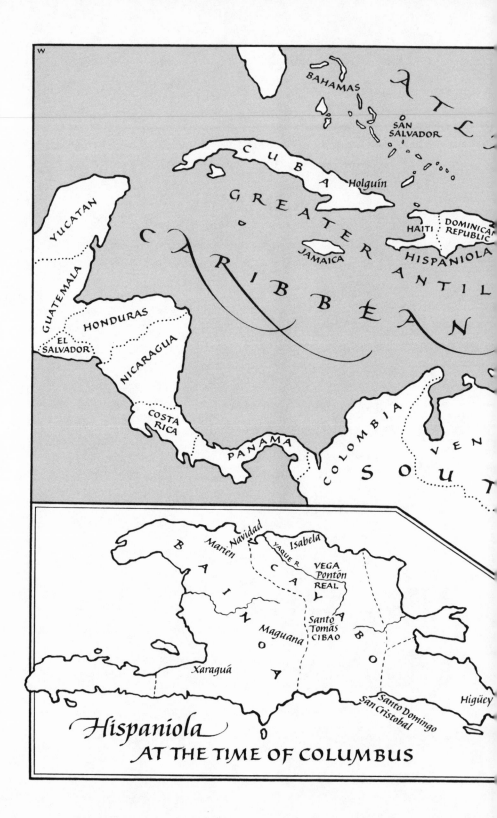

W

BAHAMAS

ATL

SAN
SALVADOR

CUBA

Holguín

GREATER

YUCATAN

C CA

RIBBEAN

JAMAICA

HAITI

DOMINICAN
REPUBLIC

HISPANIOLA

ANTIL

GUATEMALA

HONDURAS

EL
SALVADOR

NICARAGUA

COSTA
RICA

PANAMA

COLOMBIA

VEN

SOUT

C

Isabela

BAINOA

Marien

Navidad

YAQUE R

VEGA
Pontón
REAL

CAY

ABO

Santo
Tomás
CIBAO

Maguana

Xaraguá

Higüey

Santo Domingo
San Cristóbal

O

Hispaniola
AT THE TIME OF COLUMBUS

The Caribbean

ATLANTIC OCEAN

PUERTO RICO

VIRGIN ISLANDS

Anguilla

Antigua

Guadeloupe

SEA

Martinique

St. Vincent

Grenada

LESSER ANTILLES

Trinidad

ORINOCO R.

Saladero

VENEZUELA

GUYANA

SURINAM

FRENCH GUIANA

SOUTH AMERICA

BRAZIL

AMAZON R.

AMAZON R.

ORINOCO R.

Introduction

Each winter I fly south like a bird to escape the gray, icy-cold of February in New York. My paradise is Anguilla, a small island in the West Indies known for its mild, tropical climate and splendid beaches. Anguilla is near the top of a long chain of little islands that bulge out into the Atlantic Ocean to form the eastern rim of the Caribbean Sea. These islands, the Lesser Antilles, stretch from the Virgin Islands in the north down to Grenada near the coast of South America.

The peoples of the West Indies are mainly of African ancestry. Their forebears were brought to the islands during the flourishing slave trade of the sixteenth, seventeenth and eighteenth centuries. But slavery did not survive long on Anguilla. The island's rocky, arid land did not permit successful cultivation of sugar cane and a plantation economy failed to develop. The slaves were freed and forced to scratch out a meager survival or perish. As a result, their descendants, the people of Anguilla today, are particularly hearty and confident.

Anguillians are proud people steeped in the lore of the island and friendly to visitors. Over the years, I have come to know many of them and to enjoy their friendships. And so it was, one day, when a young Anguillian and I were chatting, that he chose to share a secret with me. His secret concerned an unusual cave that he had discovered. The cave was strange, he said, because ghostlike faces were carved in its walls.

My curiosity was aroused. So I asked him how I might find the cavern to see it for myself. He directed me to the site, and I found the cave at the bottom of a deep, wide hole strewn with boulders. There, on the sloping wall of the cavern, I discovered petroglyphs, pictures etched into stone—eerie, haunting spirit faces.

Who made them? Why? What did they mean?

Fascinated and curious to learn more about the faces, I revisited the cave again and again and sought information about them. I learned that the petroglyphs had been made by Indians (Amerindians or Native Americans) called Arawaks (AH ruh waks) who had lived on the island but vanished ages ago.

When I came home to New York, my interest in these Native Americans led me to museums. But there was scarcely a mention of Arawaks to be found. Instead I saw collections of Amerindian materials from the West Indies that were identified as Taino. The term Taino, I learned, is preferred by archeologists and anthropologists to identify the Native American culture that developed on the larger northern Caribbean islands, the Greater Antilles. The Tainos were the first Americans to welcome Christopher Columbus in 1492.

I began to research the Tainos. Archeologists and anthropologists have studied the pottery, tools, jewelry, religious symbols and other objects left behind by these Indians. From these artifacts, much has been learned about the Tainos' way of life. These Native Americans had no written language and left no records of their own. But the writings of Christopher Columbus and others who accompanied and followed him to the "New World" also provide a rich source of information about the Tainos. These explorers, adventurers, missionaries and colonizers described the Indians and their impressions survive in written histories and letters.

But there are no Tainos in the Caribbean today. What became of these Native Americans? This is the story of the Tainos and their mysterious fate.

CHAPTER ONE

An Ancient People

The ancestors of the Tainos lived on the grassy plains and in the surrounding lowland rain forests near the northeastern coast of South America about three thousand years ago. This area, between the great Orinoco and Amazon rivers, is part of Venezuela and the Guianas today. These ancient people were not a single tribe but a diverse family of Native Americans who spoke a common tongue that differed from the languages of other South Americans. Their language was called Arawakan and the Tainos' ancestors were known as Arawaks for this reason.

The Arawaks hunted and fished, but, most of all, they farmed. They grew a tall, leafy plant called bitter manioc, or yuca, and processed its tuberous roots to make cassava bread, the main staple of their diet. The Arawaks were skilled craftspeople who produced strong, light clay pottery of unusual quality. They created cups, bowls, jugs and other vessels which they colored red and painted with white designs. This fine, white-on-red pottery differed from that made by others and is so distinctive that it formed a telltale trail by which the Arawaks can be traced.

Although evidence of Native American life on the islands of the Caribbean had been collected and studied since the early 1900s, it was not until 1950 that the origins of the Tainos of the Greater Antilles were proven. An American archeologist, Irving Rouse, and a Venezuelan, José Cruxent, doggedly followed a buried trail of white-on-red pottery down through the chain of Caribbean islands all the way to South America. At the tiny village of Saladero in Venezuela, the trail ended. Rouse and Cruxent had discovered the origins of the Tainos and firmly connected them to their ancestors, the Arawak potters of Saladero.

Around 900 B.C., about the time King Solomon, the Israelite, was building the great temple in Jerusalem on the other side of the world, numbers of Arawaks, displaced perhaps by others who coveted their fertile lands, began to gradually leave their mainland home. Some may have ventured over land; others no doubt made their way down the Orinoco to the Atlantic coast in dugouts called "canoas." Our word canoe comes from this Arawakan term. Their emigration went on for several hundred years.

From the mouth of the Orinoco, the intrepid ancestors of the Tainos ventured out into the strong coastal current and rode it northward to the island of Trinidad. By about 190 B.C., there were at least three well-established settlements on the island. Arawaks remained on Trinidad for almost three hundred years before moving on to other islands. During this time, the Arawaks learned to adapt to this island environment. They had taken manioc cuttings with them from

South America and experimented with new ways to grow the plant; they mastered techniques for salt-water fishing. Shell-fish, crabs and sea turtles became part of their diet.

The Arawaks continued to migrate northward. They took advantage of the prevailing winds and currents to settle island after island, like so many stepping stones. Their pottery, the most reliable means of tracing the Arawak migrations, has been found on all the beautiful isles of the eastern Caribbean that comprise the Lesser Antilles: St. Vincent, Martinique, Guadeloupe, Antigua, Anguilla, the Virgins and others.

Dating the collected pottery shows that the Arawak migrations came in stages. Each new wave of settlers made its own contribution to the Arawak culture. This is shown in the changes that took place over time in their pottery. The finer type of the earlier period gradually gave way to thicker, more simply decorated pots.

The Arawak settlements appear to have prospered. But, nevertheless, the Arawaks continued to migrate northward. Why did they persist in moving on? Perhaps other Native Americans, following in their path from the mainland, harassed them and caused them to flee. Or perhaps, as their communities grew, they moved on to search for other sources of fresh water. Or simply, curiosity and the spirit of adventure may have tempted them to explore new frontiers; they could see other islands from highlands and from their canoes out at sea.

The sea was no barrier to the capable Arawaks. Even islands on the far horizon attracted them. They must have used the peaks of volcanoes on many of the islands as guideposts. During the period of their northward migration, the Arawaks formed pyramid-shaped charms from conch shells and stones. They were called "zemis" and have been

17

found only on islands where the Arawaks lived. Zemis appear to be new symbols of their great god, Yocahú, who provided not only cassava but also guided them safely across the sea.

Some Arawaks remained in the Lesser Antilles, but the migrations of many ended in the northern Caribbean. Their "promised land" was the rich, fertile islands of the Greater Antilles with plentiful rainfall, where the manioc flourished. By A.D. 300, the Arawaks had migrated about a thousand miles from their origins in South America to the northern Caribbean islands. They came first to Puerto Rico and thence westward to Hispaniola (the island consisting today of two nations: Haiti and the Dominican Republic), Cuba and Jamaica. They also ventured northward to the Bahama Islands. By A.D. 1000, when Leif Ericson and his daring Norsemen were discovering the cold, bleak shores of Newfoundland in northern North America, Arawak communities were flourishing in the northern Caribbean. The Arawak migrations had ceased.

In Cuba and in Hispaniola, called "Haiti" (meaning "Rocky") in Arawakan, the Arawaks encountered a group of island dwellers, the Ciboneys. These people were already established on these islands when the Arawaks arrived. They may have come south from Florida, east from Central America, or north from Venezuela ages before the Arawaks. The Ciboneys were food gatherers, fishers and competent stone masons, but their ways were simpler than those of the Arawaks. They lived in caves and knew nothing of pottery making or manioc cultivation. The Ciboneys withdrew into remote areas away from the Arawaks, though some may have joined the Arawaks and lived with them.

The Arawaks of these great islands passed along their

traditions to new generations, but their customs and their language changed over time. A new culture began to emerge that differed from that of their ancestors. Social scientists call this culture that developed on the islands of the northern Caribbean "Taino" to distinguish it from the earlier one that had preceded it. The word Taino in the language of these Native Americans means "good and noble people," a name they proudly used to identify themselves. The term also means "peace" and was used to greet the Europeans.

So remote were memories of their South American origins that the Tainos came to believe that the whole universe was created in the northern Caribbean, on Haiti. Myth had it that on a certain mountain on the island there were two caves. The sun and the moon were kept in one and the first people dwelled in the other. One night, the legend tells, the demon who guarded the caves chanced to slumber and the sun and the moon escaped into the sky. People also fled and came to populate the world, though some were changed by the light of the sun into trees, birds and other animals.

The Tainos lived relatively peacefully, content to fish, farm and celebrate their good fortune in festivals and worship. There were, of course, rivalries and disputes between groups and their chieftains, but the only enemies the Tainos feared were other Native Americans, the Island Caribs (from whom we get the name Caribbean).

The Island Caribs descended from earlier Arawak settlers who had remained behind in the Lesser Antilles and from Native American newcomers who continued to arrive from South America. As the blending of new immigrants into the older Arawak population of these islands continued, the nature of the society changed; it became more aggressive. Over time these people in contact with the mainland to the south differed from the Tainos living in the distant islands to the north. The term Island Carib is used to distinguish them from their Arawak forebears and from the Tainos.

The Island Caribs were skillful seamen and began to follow in the path of the earlier Arawaks. Moving steadily northward, they gradually took over island after island, attacking established Arawak settlements, killing the men and enslaving the women. By the time of Columbus's historic voyage in 1492, the Caribs had conquered all the islands of the Lesser Antilles and Carib war parties were already raiding Taino settlements in Puerto Rico and eastern Haiti.

Though stories of their warlike nature and ferocity were likely exaggerated by the Spaniards, whose histories describe the Caribs, Carib raiders were much feared by the Tainos. The training of Carib boys to become warriors began early. Carib fathers cut their sons with sharp animal teeth and put pepper in the wounds to teach their sons to bear pain. Carib men bore scars of this rite all their lives as reminders to be brave. Warriors masked their eyes with circles of black pigment before battle to terrorize their victims. They would surround unsuspecting villages under cover of darkness and swoop in at dawn to attack Taino communities with bows and poison-tipped arrows. The Caribs had no pity for their victims whom they believed to be inferior.

Ever mindful that the Carib raiders came from the sea, the Tainos preferred to live inland, away from the coastal areas that were vulnerable to Carib raids. The Tainos chose to settle on safer, higher ground from which they could warily observe the coastal waters.

CHAPTER TWO

A New Homeland

Nowhere did Taino life flourish more than in Haiti. Taino villages grew there and prospered into thriving communities. What accounted for the success of the Tainos? It was undoubtedly their resourcefulness. From the plains and lowland forests of mainland South America, they adapted to an island habitat in the Caribbean. The Tainos had no iron, so they lacked metal tools, but nevertheless, they managed to produce the implements they needed for survival primarily from stone.

The Tainos planted manioc in mounds that protected the young plants from the intense sun and prevented their crops from withering during long, dry spells. This technique provided the Tainos with a dependable and constant source of food. Manioc is grown and harvested continuously throughout the year. Its successful cultivation enabled the Tainos to settle into permanent communities unlike other people who depended upon hunting and gathering and were forced to move on whenever their food source dwindled. It is not surprising, therefore, that manioc was important in the cultural and religious life of the Tainos. Manioc was celebrated in their festivals, traditions and worship.

Haiti was settled into some five provinces. These were ruled by all-powerful chiefs, or great "caciques" (ka SEEK kays). The caciques had royal status that was passed on by birth through the mother. Though the matter is still debated, most authorities today believe that when a cacique died, his son did not usually become chief. Rather, it was likely that a nephew, a son of his wife's brother or sister, succeeded him. The children of royal birth married the offspring of other caciques to preserve royal bloodlines.

Each of the island's provinces was subdivided into districts and, in turn, into villages. These were governed by lesser caciques who directed local activities somewhat like the mayor of a town today. Taino society was not democratic. The caciques ruled and the common people had no voice in important matters.

Next in rank to the caciques was a privileged class of lesser nobility. It is not clear whether the nobles, or "nitainos," were chosen by the caciques or inherited their special positions. The nitainos participated and voted in village councils where community matters were discussed. They had the important job, for example, of determining local boundaries and fishing rights.

Priests were of the noble class. They guided religious activities and performed an important sacred ritual. In this ceremony, priests prepared a narcotic substance made from plant leaves that they ground into a powder called "cohoba." They smoked or snuffed cohoba until their minds were filled

22

with visions of zemi spirits. In this way the priests attempted to learn the will of the zemis and to foretell the future.

The common people came next in the social order. They were full-fledged members of Taino society with rights and private property. Below them was a less privileged class, the "naborias." Actual slavery did not exist in Taino communities, but the naborias were like lifelong serfs. They could not own land but worked within the villages and received maintenance in exchange for their labors.

A typical village in Haiti accommodated some two hundred to five hundred Taino families. Though caciques might have several wives and many children, the common Taino family consisted of a man, his wife and two or three children. The Tainos dwelled in very large, windowless, one-room homes. As many as fifteen families, all probably related, lived in each. The huts were sturdy and well-constructed of thatch and thick wooden posts that supported round walls and a bell-shaped roof. Each member of a Taino family had his or her own woven cotton or fiber hammock to sleep in. These were slung between the posts and rolled up during the day.

The Tainos stored cooking utensils, baskets, hollowed calabash gourds, ornaments and other household items out of the way on a wooden platform hung from the rafters above, safe from children and pets. They kept tamed parrots and small, yellow, barkless dogs. The floor of the hut was hardened earth kept immaculately clean. There was a cooking fire, some wooden stools and, often, a large, covered clay pot that held fermenting cassava from which beer was made.

The village consisted of an irregular cluster of huts located under tall shade trees. There were streets and usually a cleared open area, or plaza, surrounded by slabs of stone. The local cacique's home was set apart and faced this plaza.

The chief's home was larger than the others and spacious enough to shelter his many wives and children; it also housed the village's zemis.

Zemis were important to the rituals of the Tainos and took on different forms. The people crafted stone idols with human and animal features and made zemi dolls of cotton and wood. The Tainos believed that the zemis had spiritual powers to affect the weather, crops, sickness, childbearing and other important matters.

Each day, at sunrise, the Tainos gathered before the chief. He assigned groups of individuals to such tasks as farming, fishing, hunting and canoe building. The village priest, or shaman, was also the doctor who visited the sick. The shaman had zemi signs painted, or tattooed, on his body, and sometimes he blackened his face with charcoal. He used tobacco and medicinal herbs to heal; his chants and magic rid the ill of evil spirits.

The Tainos' principal occupation was farming. Men cleared the land, but women did most of the farm work. They cultivated the main crop, manioc, in planted fields, or "conucos," beyond the village. They grew sweet potatoes and yams among the tall manioc. These low-growing vegetables helped to prevent erosion of the manioc mounds and provided additional food for the Tainos.

The women harvested manioc by pulling the tubers up from the soil. They made cuttings from the stems which they replanted when the rains came. They carried the manioc home in baskets to each hut in the village. There they used sharpened flints to peel away the rough, brown skin of the tubers. They grated the white flesh and squeezed it through a large, finely woven sleeve to remove its poisonous juice.

Daughters helped their mothers to prepare the manioc. The girls were entertained by the women's songs and learned the stories and traditions of their people. Finally, the women baked the grated flesh, or plain meal, on clay griddles, propped up on stones, over an open fire to produce large, flat round disks of cassava bread. They then set these out to dry in the sun. Cassava bread could be stored and eaten even months later.

Corn (maize) was another crop of the Tainos. They planted it on hillsides at the time of the new moon in the belief that corn grew with the moon. Water-softened kernels were poked into the earth with a tall, pointed stick called a "dibble." Boys climbed trees to act as scarecrows, to shout and to frighten birds away when the corn ripened.

Some corn was picked while young and tender and was eaten raw; fully ripened corn was roasted. Corn bread was also produced. Women soaked the kernels in water, then pounded them with a stone pestle to make a paste that they formed into loaves. The loaves were wrapped in leaves and cooked with a little water to make the bread. Corn bread had to be eaten within a few days; unlike cassava bread which kept well, corn bread mildewed and rotted quickly. The women also made beer from corn.

Taino women kept their babies with them. Mothers carried the infants on their backs into the fields and conucos. The babies had firmly padded boards strapped to their foreheads. As the women toiled, the boards gently flattened the babies' skulls so that the Tainos grew up to have broad, flat foreheads, a fashion they found attractive.

Taino men had their tasks, too. They made seaworthy canoes, using fire, stone axes and chisels to fell great trees and to hollow them. Some of these dugouts were seventy or more feet in length and held as many as one hundred people. The Tainos used these canoes for ceremonial purposes and to travel between the islands to trade. Teams of Tainos, taking turns, paddled the gigantic dugouts great distances without the benefit of sails. The men also made smaller canoes for fishing; fish supplied much of the protein in the Tainos' diet.

The Tainos were ingenious in creating the implements they needed to catch fish. They rolled henequen plant fibers in sand to create files and saws. With these, they cut fish hooks from bone, seashell and the carapace of turtle. They formed harpoons from wood and tipped them with points of flint, bone and seashell. They twisted fibers stripped from plants into fishing line and also wove them into nets.

One of their more remarkable fishing techniques was to take a remora, or suckerfish, and let it swim out on a line from a canoe to attach itself to a sea turtle or a larger fish. When this occurred, the occupants would skillfully pull in the line and several would jump overboard to hoist in the catch. The Tainos also dove for conch in the offshore waters and, in the shallows, gathered mussels and oysters among the mangrove trees. Sometimes they captured sea turtles on the beaches or hunted their eggs in the warm sand.

They used another unusual method to fish in rivers. The stems and roots of poisonous senna shrubs were shredded and cast into a stream. When the fish snapped up this bait, the juice of the plant stunned them just long enough for boys to wade into the water and gather them in. The poison did not affect the fish for eating.

Taino men did little hunting because there was no sizeable game on the island. However, they did catch small rodents, like the rice rat and the agouti, a rabbit-sized animal, and took iguana lizards, a valued delicacy. Waterfowl, attracted to the lakes and ponds, were also prey.

Here again Taino ingenuity was apparent. The hunter would wade into a lake and partially submerge himself, wearing a decoy made from a calabash on his head. Peering out through holes cut in the gourd, the hunter would wait patiently until a curious goose approached. Then he would spring to seize its legs and capture the unlucky bird.

Boys used a different trick to catch parrots. The youngster would carry a tamed parrot up a tree, hide among the branches and wait until the pet attracted another parrot with its cries. Then, if he were quick, the boy could snatch the visitor.

Both men and women cooked the food. The men built simple grills of green sticks that burned slowly over a bed of charcoal. They broiled game and fish. They also smoked fish. Our word "barbecue" is an Arawakan term.

Women boiled down the cast-off, poisonous juice of the manioc into a thick, harmless, brown liquid into which pieces of dried cassava bread were dipped to make them soft and tasty. To this dark syrup, the women added bits of game, yams, sweet potatoes and lots of pepper to prepare a spicy stew called pepper-pot.

Women were the potters. They made the pots and griddles that were used to prepare food. They took clay from riverbeds and kneaded it with sand and water into a consistency that could be formed into coils. These ropelike coils, thick as their fingers, were mounted, one atop another, in a spiral form to create the vessel, and the inner surface was smoothed with a polished stone to join the coils, strengthen them and to make the pot watertight.

The women sometimes worked the forms of turtles, pelicans, gulls or spirit figures into the rims and added ornamental handles. They also often cut elaborate patterns into the surface of the clay with sticks. When these decorative touches were completed, they placed the pots in a shallow hole covered by flat stones and built a fire on top. Firing took many hours, but when the embers had cooled and the pots were removed, the vessels were hard and strong.

The Tainos were skilled at other handicrafts, too. They made beaded bracelets and necklaces of shell, coral and stones. Carvers produced elaborate, wooden stools called "dujos" (DO hos); these were often styled to resemble a squat animal with short legs and a raised tail for the user to lean against.

The Tainos also worked with gold. Though they placed no great value on the yellow substance, it was useful and made attractive ornaments. When they wanted gold, Taino men simply searched the gravel beds of shallow streams that flowed down from the mountains of Cibao in the central part of the island; they knew nothing of mining or digging for gold. The small, yellow nuggets they found were collected one at a time by hand. They were taken and fashioned into earrings and nose ornaments or pounded to produce foils that could be worked into ceremonial masks and belts. These pieces of jewelry and ornaments were passed down from one generation to the next.

The women, aided by their daughters, gathered cotton which grew wild in the fields and which they also cultivated. They spun the cotton into thread for hammocks or wove white fabric for skirts called "naguas" (NAG was) that only the married women wore. Most people went about naked. In the tropical climate, they must have felt comfortable. Girls also helped their mothers strip fiber from palm leaves and twist it into cord that was used for hammocks, too. A single hammock might require as much as one mile of palm cord. But so skilled were the weavers that a hammock could be produced in as little as thirteen hours.

The women wove fiber baskets which they used for cooking, carrying and storing food. Baskets also served for another purpose: the Tainos believed that spirits of the dead lived on in the skull and bones, and they often kept the remains of family members with them in covered baskets suspended from the roof of their huts or buried beneath the walls.

The bodies, or merely the heads, of certain people of particular importance might have their internal organs removed and be dried carefully over fires for preservation; some bodies were wrapped and buried for a time in shallow graves until the flesh had rotted away and the bones could be removed. Burial customs varied. Caciques might be entombed in roofed graves together with favorite wives; these women were provided with a supply of bread and water and buried alive with their husband.

The death of a cacique was a major event in the life of a Taino village and was attended by ceremonies which lasted for days. The history of the dead chief would be told in songs and dances that were performed in the village plaza.

The plaza was the center of the cultural life of the village. The Tainos had many communal leisure activities. They enjoyed a sport called "batey" (BAH tay) in which teams of men or women competed. The object of the game was to keep a rubber ball in the air by hitting it up with shoulders, elbows, hips and knees, though hands and feet could not be used. Batey was somewhat like volleyball, and it required much skill. Villagers sat on the stone slabs around the plaza to watch the games and cheer their favorites. The cacique squatted on his dujo.

The plaza was also the site of many festive occasions, for the Tainos were a happy people who loved to celebrate their good fortune. The cacique would inform his people when holidays were coming in order that they would have time to prepare. Women painted their husbands and girls decorated their brothers with black and red dyes made from plants. The men also donned colorful parrot feathers. Everyone put on strings of tinkly seashells which they tied around their arms, hips, thighs and ankles.

Songs and dances called "areytos" (a RAY tos) were part of most festivals. A leader would begin the areytos and everyone would repeat his words and copy his steps. The chanting dancers' jingling and tinkling were accompanied by the sounds of rhythmically shaken seed gourds. The cacique added to the excitement, keeping the beat with a wooden gong.

Each festival celebrated some aspect of Taino life. The areytos repeated in song and dance the tales and legends of old. Children of the village took part and learned the traditions of their people. The excitement and revelry were intoxicating, and so was the cassava beer that was consumed. The parties ended when the cacique retired satisfied and exhausted. Then everyone went home to their hammocks to rest and sleep.

For many years fortune seemed to favor this gentle people. They prospered and their culture reached new heights before the arrival of the Europeans at the end of the fifteenth century.

CHAPTER THREE

Men from Heaven

The peaceful ways of the Tainos had changed little over generations in the Greater Antilles and in the small, coral isles to the north, known today as the Bahama Islands. The Tainos of the Bahamas called themselves Lucayans. But their customs differed little from other Tainos. They, too, farmed, fished and lived in small communities ruled by caciques.

It was in the Bahamas that the Lucayans first met Europeans. The historic encounter took place on October 12, 1492 on an island the Lucayans called Guanahaní, their word for the iguanas with whom they shared it.

The strangers came in the morning, before dawn, in three great, wooden ships. The Lucayans must have been amazed by the "winged monsters," the huge vessels with their wide, white sails, that had so suddenly appeared. By Spanish accounts, the Lucayans hid in the bush and watched in awe as the enormous ships anchored in the shallow bay sent long boats toward the shore.

But curiosity must have overcome caution, for soon the Lucayans lined the beach to see bearded, white-skinned men, covered in cloth, land on the shore. The strangers displayed white flags with a large, green cross. Their chief, a tall, gray-haired man, promptly kneeled and kissed the ground. This was Christopher Columbus. His men repeated the same, strange act. Then the chief uttered a loud, foreign oath. Columbus was giving thanks to his Lord for delivering his fleet safely to this land, claiming it for Spain and naming it San Salvador.

The shy Lucayans, undoubtedly, witnessed this ritual with wonder. They must have recognized the joy of the strangers, but could not have understood what they had seen, or how it would change their lives. They timidly welcomed the visitors, convinced that these white strangers were gods dropped from Heaven.

Ironically, such was the character of Christopher Columbus who stood before the awed Lucayans that he indeed believed himself directed from Heaven. This remarkable son of a humble Genoese weaver had triumphed over the snobbish indifference of the Spanish royal court. He had by force of spirit and persistence persuaded the sovereigns, King Ferdinand and Queen Isabella, not only to sponsor this expedition but to grant him the vainglorious title "Admiral of the Ocean Sea" and a generous share of any profits the journey might produce. So the grand impression Columbus made upon the innocent Lucayans was not entirely an act, but an expression also of his supreme self-confidence.

The white men and their grand chief had come a long way. They had sailed westward across the wide ocean from Spain for thirty-three days aboard the *Niña,* the *Pinta,* and the *Santa*

María. Columbus was searching for a shorter route to the Indies, the rich exotic lands of China, Japan and India. There he anticipated finding gold, pearls, spices, gems and precious fabrics to increase the wealth of Spain. He hoped also to introduce Christianity to the peoples there.

If the Lucayans did not know what to make of the Europeans who had landed in their midst, so, too, did Columbus view the Lucayans with surprise. These natives were tall, handsome, clean-shaven people with hair trimmed above the eyes and, otherwise, cut short, except for a hank that hung down the back. Their skin was olive-tan in color and many wore face and body paint. The naked people were nothing like the prosperous Asians Columbus had expected to meet. Nevertheless, he was confident that he had reached the Indies at last. So he named the Lucayans "Indians."

The Lucayans quickly saw that this sturdy white man, with the long face and eyes the color of the sky, was respected by his men. And he was generous. He gave the Indians gifts: red caps, brass rings, tiny copper bells that tinkled sweetly and glass beads that they hung around their necks. Surely this was a good and kind God.

The Lucayans were eager to please the visitors, so they, too, brought presents. The Indians swam out to the ships with the few humble possessions they had. They gave the sailors skeins of cotton thread, darts, tamed parrots and food.

Two days later Columbus explored the island coast by boat. As he was rowed along, Lucayans on the shore followed, shouting, "Come and see the men who come from Heaven, bring them food and drink." And they did.

The Lucayans found the white chief to be friendly. But what seemed to interest him most were the little ornaments of gold that they wore in their noses and ears. The Lucayans didn't understand a word he uttered, but, through signs, they realized that Columbus wanted to find gold. They were certain that there was none on their island; the gold jewelry they possessed had been passed down to them or obtained in trade. They indicated that other islands, perhaps even a whole continent, were not far away.

Columbus needed guides to show him the way, so six Lucayans were pressed into service and taken aboard his ships. When the fleet departed, these Indians reluctantly went with it. They directed the ships to another, densely wooded island nearby. The Lucayans, however, had tricked Columbus with promises of gold in order to escape. One of them jumped overboard and swam ashore that night. Another leapt into a canoe that had come alongside and got away the next day. The Spaniards searched the island but found no gold.

Their quest for gold continued. The little fleet stopped here and there in the Bahamas. Each time the remaining guides led Columbus to expect treasure, but each time he was disappointed. The Lucayans everywhere welcomed the Europeans and generously shared their precious supplies of fresh water, filling and carrying the Spaniards' heavy casks for them.

The Indians opened their homes to the white men. They showed them sweet potatoes and maize, crops the strangers from Spain had never seen before. The Spaniards discovered the comfort of Lucayan hammocks and took several with them. So innocent were the Lucayans that they didn't realize that the guests were searching their humble huts for gold.

The Lucayans marveled at the impressive Europeans with their grand ships, colorful banners, metal armaments and amazing trinkets. With all these wonderful things, the white strangers must indeed be gods, they thought. The Lucayans tried to please the visitors, but the Spaniards mistook their good-naturedness for weakness. The Indians' favors became the strangers' expectations, and the Spaniards soon began to view the Lucayans more as servants than as equals.

Aboard the *Santa María,* his flagship, Columbus encouraged the Lucayans to participate in Christian services each sunrise and sunset. The Indians were helped to memorize the strange sounding prayers, and they learned them quickly. They kneeled and crossed themselves like the crew. Columbus began to think that the Indians might easily be converted and brought into his faith. He did not know of Yocahú and the Taino religion, or if he did, he chose to disregard it, for Columbus knew Queen Isabella's desire to convert everyone to Christianity.

The hunt for gold was not rewarded in the two weeks that the Spanish fleet spent in the Bahamas. Lucayans, however, now described a large island further to the south, and from their signs, Columbus believed that gold and pearls were to be found there. The Indians called this place "Colba" (Cuba), but Columbus was certain it was Japan. The Lucayans directed the Admiral and his ships over their age-old canoe route to Cuba, and Columbus landed on the northeast coast which had excellent natural harbors. The island was lush, green and beautiful.

By now, one of the Lucayan guides had learned some Spanish. Columbus relied on this man as an interpreter and became fond of him. Later, he would take the Indian back to Spain to be baptized and given the Christian name "Diego Colón." Diego made contact with local Tainos at stops along the coast. He told them that the Spaniards were good and generous. The Indians were pleased to trade their cotton, hammocks and food for the white men's trinkets, but it soon became apparent to Columbus that these humble people had no riches.

Many of the local Indians told Diego of a place called "Cubanacan" in the interior where gold had been found. By now, Columbus had recalculated his position, but in doing so, he had erred again. He decided that he was not in Japan but had landed, instead, at a province in China. When Diego told him about Cubanacan, Columbus believed that the Tainos were speaking of the Grand Khan, the Emperor of China. China, in fact, had no ruling emperor at that time, but Europeans did not know this.

Convinced that the Khan's palace was near, Columbus sent one of his Lucayan guides, a local Taino and two of his seamen to call upon the Emperor with a letter from the Spanish sovereigns. In hopes of communicating with the Khan, the Admiral had chosen to head the delegation a man of Jewish birth who spoke Hebrew, Aramaic and some Arabic as well as Spanish. The group set out through a fertile valley and trudged some twenty-five miles inland from the coast. They passed cultivated fields of maize, beans and sweet potatoes until they reached a village near the present city of Holguín.

This turned out to be a large Taino community—not the imperial city of China. Instead of a splendid palace, the delegation found some fifty thatched huts and about one thousand people. No grand emperor was there to greet them, only the naked cacique of the region, who received them in a gracious, though modest, way. The visitors were encouraged to squat on dujos. They were feasted and honored by a parade of curious, gift-bearing Tainos who gathered to see the messengers from Heaven. Women and children kissed the strangers' hands and feet and pressed their white skin to see if they were made of flesh and bones like themselves.

Next day the party started back to the coast. Along the way, it met some Indians engaged in a peculiar custom. The Tainos rolled leaves into a cigar, lit one end from a burning stick and inserted the other end into a nostril. Men and women inhaled the smoke from the cigar which they called a "tobaco." The Europeans were disgusted by this practice; this was the first time they had encountered smoking. The word "tobacco" comes from this Indian term for cigar.

Diego and the other Lucayan guides found almost no gold in Cuba. They were sorry to disappoint the Admiral again, but they were probably worried also that he might sail next to Haiti, which the Tainos also called "bohío" (house or home). Earlier, eager to be helpful, they had told Columbus that gold might be found there; now they regretted it. Lucayans bearing scars from brutal attacks by Carib raiders had frightened the guides. They were terrified of encountering Caribs and especially wary of visiting Haiti.

All the five weeks that Columbus explored the coast of Cuba, the Lucayans with the fleet were troubled by fears of the Caribs. On one occasion, when a party of Spaniards prepared to land, the Lucayans were so frightened that they hid below deck and could not be coaxed ashore.

Then the Lucayans' fears came true. The fleet altered course and sailed eastward. The lure of gold was to take them to Haiti after all.

CHAPTER FOUR

The Tainos' Protector

The day's sail to Haiti with Columbus was dreadful for the Lucayans. The fleet made landfall that evening of December 5.

The beauty of the island impressed the expedition as it cruised along the northwestern coast. The land so reminded the Admiral of Spain that he named the island "La Isla Española" (The Spanish Isle, present-day Hispaniola). He claimed the island for the Spanish Crown in a brief ceremony on the shore and raised a great cross there.

This ritual must have meant nothing to the curious Tainos who gathered to gape at the wondrous visitors. They probably sat quietly on their heels, which was their greeting to signify peace. The golden ornaments the Indians wore and their lack of weapons, however, did not escape notice by the strangers. The local cacique, a young man about twenty-one years old, greeted the white men. Perhaps he found it reassuring to meet Diego and the other Lucayans in Columbus's party. The cacique accepted an invitation to dine with the Admiral aboard his flagship.

That evening the naked young chieftain, accompanied by counselors, was a guest of the Admiral. He sat with Columbus in his cabin and politely tasted a bit of Spanish food and drink. Then he graciously presented his host with gifts: a belt and two pieces of hammered gold. In return, he received a bottle of orange water, red shoes and a necklace of amber beads that the Admiral took from around his own neck. The cacique was further honored when he departed. A seaman piped, or blew a whistle, as the cacique left. This naval courtesy signaled the departure of a person of rank. An impressive volley of cannon fire, a further salute, followed. The chief was rowed to shore and carried away upon the shoulders of his men seated on a litter.

But if the young cacique and his people believed that the Spaniards were prepared to treat them with continued respect, they were wrong. For in his journal that very night, Columbus wrote of how easy it would be to conquer and enslave the Indians. He boasted that with his crew (ninety men) he ". . . could overrun all these islands without opposition . . . [for the Indians] bear no arms, and are all unprotected and so very cowardly that a thousand would not face three; so they are fit to be ordered about and made to work. . . ."

Tainos living along the coast learned about the generous white visitors quickly, as Columbus hoped they might. The Indians received the white men eagerly and showered them with gifts of cassava bread, calabashes of fresh water and fruits. Seeing evidence of gold, the Spaniards' lust to find the precious metal intensified. The Tainos were questioned about the origin of their ornaments but could only indicate that the gold came from an area to the east. So the fleet made ready to sail further eastward.

Just at this time Guacanagarí, the cacique of the densely populated district of Marien, to the east of Columbus's anchorage, sent a messenger to the Admiral. He had received word of Columbus and wished to meet the great white cacique. Guacanagarí, who was the ruler of much of northwestern Hispaniola, invited Columbus to visit and sent him an extraordinary gift. This was a belt about four fingers wide, embroidered in red and white with fishbones. The center of the belt formed a mask, a face with ears, nose and tongue made of hammered gold. The gift was a sign of welcome, a token in the Taino tradition, that the cacique wished to receive the white chief peaceably, with honor, as an equal. Columbus accepted Guacanagarí's invitation but he cautiously sent a patrol off in a boat to learn the way and to determine that it was safe. His men were gone for two days and nights.

During their absence, the *Santa María* had many guests. So many Tainos clambered aboard the flagship that a constant party atmosphere must have prevailed. Feeling welcome, the Indians visited day and night, bearing gifts, eager to meet the white strangers and to explore the ship. As many as fifteen hundred Tainos may have paddled or swam out to board the vessel, though it was anchored some three miles from shore. Any Indian who seemed likely to have information was questioned about the gold.

When the patrol returned from Guacanagarí's village, it told Columbus that the way was safe and that the cacique's subjects were eager to receive him. But the news that excited the Admiral most was word of the mountainous central part of the island, the Cibao, where gold lay waiting. As fate would have it, in his eagerness, Columbus assumed that this Indian word was a mispronunciation of "Cipango," the name which the explorer Marco Polo, almost two hundred years earlier, had given Japan. Columbus now believed that, at last, he was on the path to that fabled, golden empire. In reality, his emissaries had repeated the word "Cibao" correctly.

On December 24, the expedition set out for Guacanagarí's harbor, which was less than a day's sail away. But the wind suddenly died and the ships were becalmed. That night, the sailor on watch drowsed, tired perhaps, from the exhausting partying of the previous days. Disaster struck. The *Santa María* had drifted slightly in the ebbing evening tide and come to rest upon a sandbar from which it could not be freed. Stuck in the sand, grounded, the strained timbers of the ship creaked, groaned and split apart. The wooden hull began to break up.

Columbus ordered crewmen into a boat to tow the stricken ship free, but in a cowardly way they rowed away to the *Niña* instead. Turned back by the *Niña,* the men finally attempted to pull the *Santa María* free, but it was too late. The sea poured into the damaged ship and by daybreak the situation was hopeless.

Now every effort was directed to salvaging the ship's provisions and supplies. Men were dispatched to ask for Guacanagarí's help, and the cacique sent his people to assist the desperate sailors. The Tainos rescued the ship's stores, including biscuits, salted meat and fish, olive oil, wine, beans, dried peas, nuts and rice. They saved weapons, tools, seeds, line, fishing tackle, other equipment and trading cargo and took them safely to shore.

Columbus was surprised and relieved that none of these materials was stolen by the Indians. But the Admiral was distraught, nonetheless, by loss of his ship. Observing his distress, Guacanagarí made efforts to console the white chief. He provided two generous huts to house the Spaniards and their goods. He also gave the shipwrecked Admiral encouragement that he could indeed find the gold he sought in Cibao.

Hearing about the gold must have helped to restore Columbus. He presented Guacanagarí with a shirt and a pair of gloves and invited him to dine aboard the *Niña* which he was now using as his flagship. The cacique, in turn, made a feast for Columbus. Lobsters, roast agouti, yams, sweet potatoes, cassava bread and other foods were prepared and cooked on the beach. With the aid of interpreters and signs, the two chiefs communicated at length.

Guacanagarí spoke of the dangers his people faced from the Caribs. The Taino farmers, armed only with short darts tipped with fish-tooth points, were all but defenseless against their enemy's bows and arrows. The cacique's unselfishness and his genuine concern for his people gave Columbus an idea. He ordered his men to demonstrate their weaponry. They shot their powerful bows, discharged muskets and fired different types of cannon. It was an impressive, if scary, display for the Indians.

Now Columbus proposed his plan. The Spaniards would construct a fort here, and they would stay and protect their friends, the Tainos, from attack by the Caribs. Guacanagarí saw the advantage in having such powerful allies to defend his people and accepted the apparently generous offer. The idea for the first European settlement in America since the Norsemen visited was born.

Later that night Columbus mused about the gold, Cibao and the shipwreck. So convinced of his exalted role and mission in life was the Admiral of the Ocean Sea that even in

42

this adversity he found special significance. It is God's will, not ill-fortune, that guides my destiny, he decided.

He ordered his men to take timbers and planks from the wrecked *Santa María* and build a fort on the shore. The sweet-tempered Tainos did much of the carting and heavy work. When the fort was completed, Columbus named it "La Navidad" (Christmas) to commemorate the time of the shipwreck. He chose thirty-nine seamen to remain behind to garrison the fort. The men were to find a suitable place for a permanent settlement and continue the search for gold while he would return to Spain to proclaim his success and to prepare another expedition. The Spaniards were to treat the Indians kindly while he was away.

Columbus decided to take Diego, some other Taino guides and Indian artifacts back with him aboard the *Niña* to show the sovereigns. He informed Guacanagarí of his plans to journey home for more supplies and promised to return. The two men, now friends, feasted, embraced and said their farewells on January 2, 1493. The cacique had become so fond of Columbus, the Tainos' new protector, that the Admiral's departure grieved him.

CHAPTER FIVE

Gold Fever

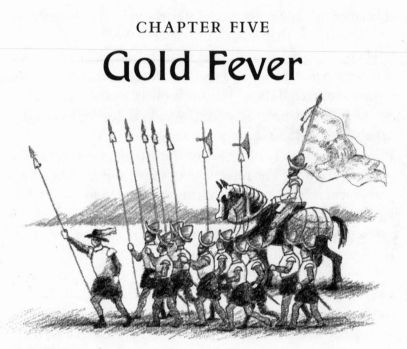

In Spain, Columbus enjoyed the glorious welcome of a hero. He triumphantly announced his discoveries. Proudly he displayed the gold objects collected in the Indies and paraded Diego and the other Tainos before the sovereigns. The gentle Indians charmed Queen Isabella as Columbus had hoped. The Admiral had already suggested to the deeply religious Queen that the Indians could easily be brought to Christianity, an idea that appealed greatly to the sovereign, and, with her and King Ferdinand's approval, Diego and the other Indians were baptized and given Christian names.

Now the sovereigns asked Pope Alexander VI to recognize their claim to the newly discovered lands. The Pope, who was of Spanish birth, granted Spain dominion over the new territories, but solely on condition that the natives there be converted to the Holy Faith.

Though Columbus had not reached Japan or China, he excited the King and Queen with accounts of his discoveries in the Indies and promised them heaps of gold to pay for future expeditions and to swell the royal treasury. With his sovereigns' support, Columbus assembled ships and supplies for a second, even larger, expedition. It sailed to the Indies in late September 1493.

The Spanish fleet anchored off Hispaniola on November 27. Word of its arrival reached Guacanagarí and alarmed him. There was reason for his concern. In the period of Columbus's absence much had happened and none of it would please the Admiral. The fort at Navidad had been destroyed and its garrison killed.

Guacanagarí knew that Columbus would quickly discover the destruction at Navidad and the fate of its men. He feared that he would be blamed and that the Spanish, with their powerful weapons, would seek revenge against him. So the wily chief made excuses and delayed meeting Columbus. The Admiral, however, would not be put off and came to Guacanagarí.

The cacique pretended to be injured; he wore a bandage on his thigh. Guacanagarí claimed to have suffered a wound fighting to defend the ill-fated garrison and the fort and told Columbus what had happened. Historians are skeptical about his story, because caciques were known to invent tales to flatter themselves and to increase their prestige at the expense of rival chiefs. But it is the only account of what might have happened.

According to Guacanagarí, the good feelings between the Tainos and the Spaniards began to break down after Columbus had departed. The Admiral's promise of friendship and protection of the Tainos was soon betrayed by the men he had left behind. The garrison had become undisciplined and quarrelsome. Gangs from the fort made raids upon Taino villages and abused the local peoples.

Finally, in a central district known as Maguana, a rival cacique was provoked to fight the sailors. This chief, Caonabo (KAY oh nah bo), along with others, then led an attack on Navidad. The fort was burned and the garrison hunted down and killed. Out of loyalty to their friendship, so the story went, Guacanagarí had attempted unsuccessfully to defend the Spaniards and had been wounded in the struggle.

Columbus decided to accept the cacique's account though he was not taken in by the feigned wound. He believed Guacanagarí if not entirely truthful, to be essentially innocent, of participating in the destruction of the fort and its garrison. He defended the cacique against those of his expedition who urged that Guacanagarí be executed as a warning to the Tainos. Besides, Columbus knew that the cacique's help would be essential in furthering his own plans. Columbus's attitude toward the Tainos may have hardened as a result of what had happened, but he decided against taking any immediate revenge. He would settle his score with Caonabo in due course.

Now, once again, the Tainos were impressed by the power and splendor of the Spanish. The great white chief had returned with a huge fleet of seventeen ships laden with wondrous things: tools and equipment, supplies of strange materials and foods, unusual plants and seeds, livestock and huge creatures called horses.

The Spaniards, more than twelve hundred strong, had come prepared to build a permanent colony in the Indies. The Tainos watched as the newcomers promptly set about constructing a settlement. Had they been asked, the Indians might have advised the white men not to build on the site

46

Columbus had hastily selected. It was an infertile, barren place that lacked water suitable for drinking. Its harbor was poor and was infested with mosquitoes. But the Spaniards were arrogant, and the timid Tainos were not consulted.

The Indians observed with fascination as a European town was built. Columbus named it Isabela for the Spanish Queen. Unlike the humble Taino villages, the town was laid out in a typically European design. Facing the plaza were a church and Columbus's own residence. This was a particularly large stone house, a novel form of construction to the Indians.

The Tainos, who had farmed the land successfully for centuries, could have shown the Spanish how to create conucos to grow manioc, sweet potatoes and yams, which flourished in the local soil. But again they were not asked. So they sat on their heels and watched the white men sow fields of wheat and plant grapevines, crops more suitable to the soil and climate of Spain. Perhaps they thought that the confident Spaniards possessed greater wisdom and knew what they were doing.

It was only a matter of days, however, before the Indians saw that the settlers were in serious trouble. Ignoring their poor condition from the long sea journey, Columbus had ordered his men to work too quickly. They lacked sufficient stamina for the labors he required of them. The tropical climate drained their strength, and they fell victim to exhaustion and thirst. The poor water they drank from the local wells only added to their misery. The malarial mosquitoes began to affect them also, and they took sick with chills and fevers. The Spaniards' plight became more desperate, day by day, as their rations dwindled.

The Tainos began to realize that the Spaniards were not gods, but mortals, after all. They felt compassion for the stricken colonists and brought fish and yams to feed the starving settlers. But, even in their distress, the Spanish continued to ask about gold.

Why the white men so desperately sought gold must have puzzled the Tainos, who had prospered and lived contentedly for ages without placing great value on the yellow substance. But the Spanish seemed to crave gold the way a fevered person thirsts for water; it was as if the white men had a gold fever.

Even as the settlers struggled to survive and to build a town, Columbus sent one of his most competent young captains, Alonso de Hojeda, to lead a troop into the interior in search of gold. Indians willingly guided the Spaniards to the mountain streams of Cibao where gold was to be found. Along the route, other Tainos, told of the quest, generously gave the visitors what gold they possessed.

Hojeda brought the gold he obtained back to Columbus. The Admiral was encouraged, but he needed more, much more gold, to convince the sovereigns to continue supporting his mission. The colony at Isabela was barely able to manage even with the generous help of the Indians. Columbus urgently needed supplies from Spain: medicines for the hundreds of sick men, food, livestock, clothing, footwear and also miners who could advise his men how to extract the precious ore. Twelve ships were to return to Spain, so Columbus sent Hojeda's gold along with them.

Determined to find more gold, the Admiral decided now to lead the search himself. So he assembled a grand procession of hundreds of troops in armor, on foot and on horseback and led them deep into the island. The Indians must have gaped wide-eyed with wonder as the Spaniards with their tools and weapons and banners and trumpets marched by.

The force crossed a wide, green beautiful valley which so impressed Columbus that he named it "La Vega Real" (The Royal Plain). The Tainos knew this land as Cayabo (or Magua), the domain of the great cacique, Guarionex. Years before the arrival of Columbus, Guarionex's father had received a troubling prophecy from the zemi. It predicted the coming of strangers, covered in cloth, who would attack the Tainos and conquer them.

But the Admiral and his men were not hostile toward the Indians and the Tainos did not resist their passage. In fact they did all they could to be hospitable and to assist the Spaniards. They gave them gifts of food and gold and helped the troops to ford a river in their path at the village of Pontón.

The expedition made its way into the wild mountains of Cibao. There Columbus directed his men to construct a fort, which he named Santo Tomás, to protect future mining operations. From the surrounding hills and valleys, Tainos came to Santo Tomás to see the great chief of the white men. Again they brought gifts of food and gold to celebrate his visit. Columbus assigned a garrison under the command of a Spanish nobleman named Pedro Margarite to remain behind and protect the base.

Weary, no doubt, from the long return march to Isabela, Columbus was not pleased to find disorder and near-mutiny when he arrived. He had left the stronghold in the command of his youngest brother, Diego. But the task of controlling the hundreds of noblemen, adventurers, soldiers and workers was beyond the peaceable Diego. Bored, ill, hungry and homesick after three hard months away, the impatient colonists no longer had faith in promises of gold and wealth.

Mere words would not appease the disgruntled men; their mood was ugly and their attitude was menacing. These Spanish hidalgos, or noblemen, harbored considerable resentment toward Columbus. Never truly accepted by them, this Italian of humble origin who behaved in so arrogant a manner was regarded with contempt. Admiral of the Ocean Sea indeed, they scoffed; nothing might have pleased them more than to see Columbus humiliated and brought low.

Columbus sensed a serious threat in their hostility. So cleverly he devised a plan to ease this dangerous situation. He would divide his forces and send half of them, including the rabble-rousers, under Alonso de Hojeda to Santo Tomás. Some of these men would relieve the garrison and remain at the fort. Pedro Margarite would then lead the greater number on a mission to explore the countryside.

CHAPTER SIX

Homeless in Their Own Land

On April 9, 1494, the expedition to Santo Tomás left Isabela under the stern command of Alonso de Hojeda. No doubt Columbus had chosen this captain to lead the restless, unruly troops because of Hojeda's reputation for toughness and daring. He was a clever man with a quick, cruel temper, likely to be obeyed by those he led.

On the march, the captain was angered by rumors that the Indians, who had helped Columbus's men to ford the river at Pontón earlier, had made off with some clothing. These clothes were now said to be in the possession of the local cacique. When Hojeda reached the area, he captured the chief and took his brother, nephew and one of the nitainos prisoner also.

The terrified Indians were taken to their village plaza. There, as the Tainos watched in horror, Hojeda viciously cut off the ears of the respected nitaino. The mutilated victim, the cacique and the others were then taken away in chains to Isabela and brought before Columbus.

If the bewildered and frightened prisoners had hoped for mercy from the white chief, none was forthcoming. The Admiral ordered that they be beheaded. But another cacique who had helped Columbus could not stand by and let the Indians die. He bravely confronted the Admiral and begged him to spare the captives. Columbus relented. Because he was indebted to this chief, he let the prisoners go free.

Meanwhile, the Tainos in the Vega must have been happy to see the ruthless Hojeda and his troops move on. But the peace that followed their departure proved to be short-lived, for the garrison at Santo Tomás relieved by Hojeda joined up with the new force and returned to the Vega now under the command of Margarite. The troops, already ill-humored, were further irritated by meager rations, for Columbus had had few provisions to spare the expedition. His orders had been for the Spaniards to obtain the food they needed from the Indians. The stage was set for trouble.

Though the Admiral had directed that the Tainos be treated kindly and with respect, he had turned loose an army of hungry soldiers. The Spaniards swept across the once tranquil plains like a plague of swarming locusts, leaving ruin and famine in their path. Taino villages were sacked, and the little food stored in their huts was taken. The oppressed Tainos fled their villages, abandoned their carefully cultivated conucos and became refugees in their own land.

While this rampage was taking place in the spring and summer of 1494, Columbus visited the island of Jamaica to search for gold; he was unsuccessful. He also returned to Cuba to explore more of its coastline. The Admiral hoped to prove that Cuba was not just another island, but part of the mainland of Asia. He cruised westward along the southern coast of Cuba for more than a month without finding the sought-for landmass. Finally he had had enough. Without going further, he determined nonetheless that Cuba was a Chinese province, a peninsula that would join the Asian mainland ahead to the west. To silence any doubters later on, he compelled his crew to sign statements supporting his claim. The sailors were warned that anyone who might disagree in the future would be fined severely and have his tongue cut out.

Columbus returned to Hispaniola at the end of September to discover the undisciplined brutality toward the Indians that was taking place. He appointed his newly arrived brother, Bartolomé, commander of all Spanish forces. Columbus gave Bartolomé, who was devoted to him, the title "El Adelantado" (The Leader) and directed him to restore order.

By this time, however, relations between the Spanish and Tainos had become a serious problem. The Spanish depended upon the Indians to supply their food, but many Tainos had fled their homes and conucos and there was hunger on the island. The Tainos suffered most; an estimated fifty thousand of them would perish before year's end. The ancient Taino civilization and the simple farming economy on which it depended were being destroyed by the Europeans, who, for all their advantages and arrogance, failed to understand the disastrous consequences of their greed.

The Tainos were beginning to suffer in increasing numbers, also, from the introduction of foreign diseases. These imported Old World killers included smallpox, yellow fever, plague, measles and influenza. Carried by the Spaniards, these epidemic diseases now attacked the vulnerable Tainos who lacked immunity to them.

Although the plight of the colonists, whose supplies were running out, was temporarily relieved when four caravels arrived from Spain, still the ravaging of the central districts of the island persisted. Margarite, insulted by criticism of the conduct of his troops, left Hispaniola and sailed for Spain. His soldiers, abandoned by their commander, now became renegades and continued to harass and to terrorize the Indians in the central districts. The rampage went on, unabated, into 1495. The tormented Indians continued to flee this brutality; they hid, starving in the rugged countryside.

Finally matters became so unbearable that the Tainos struck back. The Indians raided a fort that the Spanish had built at the Yaque River in the Vega. They attacked the garrison and killed ten of the Spanish defenders.

The attack alarmed Columbus. His forces, though better armed, were greatly outnumbered. If the Indians were to unite, they might overrun the Spanish. But centuries of wars had provided the Europeans with military advantages in tactics, armor and weaponry, and Columbus used them.

The Tainos were no match for the Spaniards who had armor, steel lances, swords, deadly crossbows and small caliber firearms called arquebuses. The Indians were easily routed. The Spanish cavalry pursued and captured them.

If conquering the Tainos did not prove difficult for Columbus, however, finding gold enough to pay the costs of his expedition did. How was he to keep his promises of wealth to the sovereigns in Spain? The quantity of gold he had managed to collect thus far was wholly inadequate.

The Admiral's ingenuity once again provided an answer. Though earlier, Columbus had won favor with the Queen by showing the Tainos to be generous, peaceful people who might easily be converted to Christianity, he now schemed to betray the Indians to satisfy his debts. There were many

Indian captives from the recent battle. Instead of releasing them, he planned to ship the Taino prisoners in bondage to Spain. There, in the slave market in Seville, they would fetch profits to pay the expenses of his enterprise.

So some sixteen hundred luckless Taino captives were rounded up and taken to the port at Isabela. The great white chief who they had welcomed and treated as a god had turned on them and become a demon.

Only five hundred fifty of the captives, however, could be jammed into the dark, dank holds of the four caravels returning to Spain. So "the best males and females," like prize cattle, were selected for shipment. Others were held as slaves to the colonists in Isabela. The Spanish adventurers who had come to Hispaniola acted now as though they were privileged gentlemen who were above working with their hands. The remaining captives were released and ran off as far as they could go, traveling even seven or eight days to find refuge in the hills and forests.

The Indians taken aboard the Spanish vessels fared miserably, huddled naked in the dark, smelly depths of the ships without warmth or adequate sanitation. Almost half of them perished and were thrown overboard during the stormy crossing. Those who survived to reach Spain were in such poor condition that most died soon afterward.

Behind them, the oppression on Hispaniola continued. The Spanish realized, by now, that they could rule the Indians more easily by controlling or removing the caciques. Chief Guatiguaná, who was responsible for the death of the ten Spanish soldiers at the Yaque River fort, and two lesser caciques were captured, bound and taken to Isabela to be executed. But the resourceful prisoners managed to chew through each other's bonds during the night and get away.

Guatiguaná now tried to rally his people to fight the

invaders. He hoped to unite the demoralized Indians and drive the Europeans into the sea. He spoke to Guacanagarí, but despite the Spanish brutalities, he could not turn the cacique from his loyalty to his friend Columbus. Guatiguaná also tried to arouse the great caciques in the southwest and southeast of the island. But they had been unaffected so far by the havoc in the central territory and would not stir their peoples to fight in a war they hoped to avoid.

So Guatiguaná courageously recruited an army on his own. But before the Indians could organize and attack, they were struck first by the Admiral, Bartolomé and Hojeda. Guatiguaná's forces were beaten by a well-armed troop of two hundred infantry with vicious, trained attack dogs and cavalry, accompanied by Guacanagarí and some of his men.

Caonabo, the bold cacique who had allegedly destroyed the fort at Navidad, remained at large, however, and still posed a threat to the colonists. So Hojeda devised a clever trap to capture him. He and a small group were sent to find Caonabo, pretending to be on a friendly mission.

Caonabo received Hojeda peacefully at his home in Maguana and was told that Columbus wished to meet him in Isabela. The cacique was invited to ride there on horseback befitting a chief of his importance and to wear ornaments such as a king of Spain might do. Honored, Caonabo took the bait and accepted the offer. He was helped up onto Hojeda's horse and he permitted the Spaniards to place metal bracelets on his wrists and ankles.

These "royal ornaments" were actually cleverly disguised handcuffs and shackles. Once they were in place, the clasps were snapped closed; the trap was sprung. Surprised and helpless, Caonabo discovered the treachery too late. He was tied back to back to Hojeda to keep him from falling and taken away to Isabela to prison, where he remained until the following year when he was put aboard a ship for Spain. The once proud chief, defeated by trickery, was the first cacique to be eliminated by the Spaniards; he died at sea.

Other caciques rose up to defend their people and land, but none was strong enough to defeat the Spaniards. One by one they fell or were captured. Behechio, the powerful chief of Xaraguá, a district in the southwest, marched into the Cibao and fought hard there, but he, too, was captured although he later escaped. The Indians fought for the better part of a year, from May 1495 to March 1496, before they were finally crushed.

The Tainos in the central districts were now completely dispirited, and Columbus moved to take cruel advantage of them. He imposed a severe tax upon every Indian male fourteen years of age or older living in the Cibao and the Vega. Every three months, or four times a year, each man was required to provide a quantity of gold dust, sufficient to fill a small copper bell (about one-half to three-quarters of an ounce) or be put to death. Tainos in districts not known to have gold were to give twenty-five pounds of cotton instead.

To ensure that the tribute was paid, each Indian was made to wear a tag around the neck. This was stamped as a form of receipt to show that the tax had been collected. The local caciques were forced to oversee the heartless program and armed Spaniards, operating from a number of newly built forts, enforced it.

Not only was the tax inhuman but it was ill-conceived. The Spanish had already taken, or extorted, virtually all the gold the Indians had managed to collect over generations on the island. This gold had been gathered casually from the gravelly shallows of streams, and the Tainos knew nothing more of its origins or how to dig for it.

The great cacique, Guarionex, tried to persuade Columbus to lift the unbearable tribute. Instead of the tax, he offered to cultivate a tract of land from the north shore clear across the island to the south coast, a conuco that could have more than fed all the Spanish colonists. But the Admiral, determined to pay his debts to the sovereigns in gold, foolishly rejected the offer. He consented, however, to halve the tax.

The Tainos suffered horribly under the tribute. They found themselves in a terrible trap. On one hand, the Indians faced starvation. On the other, they faced death if they failed to provide the required tax. So, many Tainos gave up everything and fled to the mountains. Homeless in their own land, they were hunted down like animals by the Spaniards. Numbers of Indians decided to take their own lives rather than submit to the white man's tyranny. They committed suicide, deliberately drinking raw, poisonous cassava juice. Those who tried to resist the oppressors were tortured and killed.

During the four years that followed the arrival of Columbus, the Taino population of Hispaniola was devastated by abuse, starvation and most of all, disease. Archeological and historical evidence leads experts today to believe that the Taino population of Hispaniola was about one million when Columbus first arrived in 1492. By 1496, a third of these native people had perished.

CHAPTER SEVEN

The Blood Tax

The tribute was an oppressive burden from which the Tainos under Spanish control could find no escape but death; it was a blood tax. The caciques were forced to obey the Spaniards. The only way to save their people seemed to lie in cooperating with the oppressors in the hope that the white men would soon learn that the tribute was unrealistic.

Guarionex commanded his subchiefs to collect the tribute in gold as he was required to do. But these lesser caciques had increasing difficulties obtaining it from their subjects. The Indians hated the Spanish by now; the strangers whom they had welcomed to their land, had, through brutality and force, become their masters. Nevertheless, the caciques made efforts to gather the tribute, even using tricks to collect it. In one village, a desperate chief was known to have rigged a tube to a hollowed idol so that an assistant could call out to his people in the voice of the zemi for the offensive tax.

The Tainos must have called upon their gods for relief from the burden of the tribute. Their pleas may have seemed answered when, in 1496, the Adelantado was convinced to follow some Tainos southward away from the Vega. According to one account, a Spaniard had heard, from a Taino woman with whom he lived, about a new site said to have gold. Another story was that Guarionex told Bartolomé about a new gold field, hoping to divert the Spaniards from the Vega. Whatever the case, Taino guides led the Adelantado through the Cibao mountains to a place where gold was found. Columbus later proudly called this site San Cristóbal, to honor the patron saint for whom he was named.

Excited by the promise of riches at the new site, the Adelantado decided to move his base closer to the goldfield. As the Indians had known all along, Isabela was a terrible location for the Spaniards to have settled in the first place. So Bartolomé energetically set out and found a suitable harbor on the southeast coast of the island. There, about thirty miles from San Cristóbal, he began to construct a new capital, a settlement to be called Santo Domingo which was destined to become an important city.

But any Taino expectations that the new goldfield would ease their oppression by the Spaniards were disappointed. It did not cause the Spaniards to remove the tribute, and so their miseries were not relieved. Indeed, the construction of Santo Domingo seemed to end any hopes that the white men would lose interest in the Tainos' now wretched land and leave the island.

In March 1496, Columbus returned to Spain and left Bartolomé behind in charge of the colony. Months later, a letter from the Admiral arrived, advising the Adelantado that a religious controversy in Spain about the enslavement of the Indians had been resolved. It was decided that making slaves of the Tainos was acceptable only if the Indians were taken as prisoners of war. In other words, it was necessary only to accuse the Tainos of fighting back in order to deprive them of their freedom.

So now it became a deliberate policy of the colonists to incite the Indians to resist mistreatment in order to arrest and condemn them to slavery. Three hundred Tainos were immediately accused and convicted of rebellious or warlike acts by the Adelantado and promptly shipped off to Spain to be sold into lifetime slavery.

The Adelantado was an able, stern and powerful leader. In sole command of the colony now and emboldened, perhaps, by his successful enterprise on the southeast coast at Santo Domingo, he was eager to enlarge his domain.

Until 1496, the Spanish had confined their presence to the central districts of the island, principally to Cayabo province. But now the Adelantado marched his troops westward to the river which marked the boundary between Cayabo and the province of Bainoa. He was met here by Behechio, the great cacique of the southwest.

Behechio was aware that the Adelantado was coming and had decided to receive him peacefully. Knowing that his province did not produce gold and that his people could not possibly satisfy the Spanish demand for it, he hoped to avoid the gold tax. Could he, by friendly persuasion, convince Bartolomé to accept tribute of another kind?

So Behechio greeted the Adelantado with a guard of honor and complimented the Spanish with a great show of respect. Behechio's efforts succeeded. Bartolomé agreed to accept cotton, hemp and cassava in place of the gold tribute. Relieved, the cacique brought the Adelantado and his troops through the forested and mountainous province to his home in Xaraguá.

Xaraguá was a great, arid plain made fertile by a system of irrigation ditches. The Tainos diverted water from a river through these canals to fields where cotton grew in abundance. The Indians of Xaraguá were the most respected Tainos of the island. They were admired for their cultural activities, polished speech and refinement.

Behechio lived in a large, round hut, or "caney," with his thirty wives and children. It was a palace by Taino standards. Behechio's sister, Queen Anacaona, shared power with the cacique in Xaraguá. She was the widow of the heroic chief, Caonabo, who had fallen to Spanish treachery. Anacaona was a lovely, gracious woman admired and renowned for her great talent in creating songs and dances for the areytos.

If Anacaona harbored any hatred for the Spanish, she concealed it well during the Adelantado's visit. Perhaps the stakes were too great for any display of personal bitterness. For three days, she and Behechio entertained their guests royally, treating them to feasts, dances and games. These sporting contests with bows and arrows were so daring that several Indians were killed competing in the events. The Adelantado was impressed, and the visit was a success. But Behechio and Anacaona had agreed to pay a ransom in return for peace.

When the payment was ready, the Adelantado returned to Xaraguá. This time he came by ship. The tribute had been collected by thirty-two local caciques, and the Indians had kept their part of the bargain. Anacaona kept up her effort to please Bartolomé and retain his friendship by presenting him with gifts. She gave him, among other things, fourteen beautifully carved dujos of polished, black wood. The Adelantado seemed delighted and rewarded Anacaona and Behechio with a tour of his ship and a brief sail offshore.

But if there was peace in the western province, the central districts, especially the Vega, remained in chaos. The caciques could not extract the tribute from their overburdened peoples. Now, more than ever, they saw the futility of trying to collect the senseless tax. Their only hope to free their people from the Spanish yoke was to fight the oppressors. The caciques pushed Guarionex to be their leader and planned to assemble an army of fifteen thousand men. The day the Spanish were to collect the tax was when the Tainos would strike.

Guarionex had an alliance with a Spanish official named Francisco Roldán. Roldán had been appointed chief justice of the island by Columbus, but he was discontented and ambitious. He plotted to kill the Adelantado and to take over the island while the Admiral was still away in Spain. Roldán promised Guarionex that he would lift the burden of the tribute from the Indians if the chief would join forces with him and his seventy or so followers in their rebellion against Bartolomé.

Guarionex, more desperate than ever now to ease the plight of his people, placed his trust in Roldán and agreed to support him. But word of the plan to attack the Spanish leaked out and reached the Adelantado, who reacted quickly. Before the Indian forces could organize, Bartolomé's troops swooped down upon the Tainos' villages in a swift, nighttime raid. The caciques were caught asleep in their hammocks and rounded up. The uprising was ended before it could begin.

Fourteen caciques were captured in the stunning raid. They were taken to the Adelantado at a fort in the Vega. Two were condemned to death and later, executed. The others, including Guarionex, were threatened with severe punishment if they rebelled again and were released. This action was more a matter of practicality than a gesture of compassion. The Spanish feared that without caciques to keep their communities intact the Tainos would continue to abandon their farms in increasing numbers. The Indians had already shown that they were prepared to starve in order to deprive the Spanish of food.

Guarionex returned to the Vega. No doubt, he felt discouraged and powerless. Perhaps the terrible prophecy revealed to his father years before was on his mind. For had not the zemi predicted all that was happening? Strangers had come. They were not naked, painted Caribs who raided and then withdrew. They were powerful intruders who wore clothes, and resisting them was hopeless. Guarionex and his people knew now that the strangers of the prophecy were Christopher Columbus and his Spanish forces. Was there no way to be rid of them and the famine and death they had brought?

Roldán, in whom Guarionex had placed his confidence, turned out to be no more honorable than the other Spaniards. He and his men also plundered and abused the Tainos, and the tribute remained. The cacique's faith in Spanish promises was over. Guarionex could no longer bear his people's suffering. For two years, he had tried and failed to help them. Now he would turn elsewhere for aid. He took his family and left to seek refuge with Mayobanex, the cacique of the territory to the north of the Vega.

This was the rugged, mountainous land of the Macorix. These Indians were of mixed blood, both Taino and Carib. They were considered Tainos but had their own distinctive language and customs. They wore their long, coarse hair tied behind their head in a net of parrot feathers and were more aggressive than other Taino clans. They fought with bows and arrows and were more warlike. In them, Guarionex found an ally with whom he could attack the Spanish. He organized a force of Macorix warriors and made several successful raids against the Spanish who had moved in and taken over Taino villages on the fertile plains below.

When Columbus returned to Hispaniola at the end of August 1498, the Indian raids so threatened the security of the Spanish that one of the first things he did was to order the Adelantado and a troop of soldiers to stop the mounting violence. But when the Spanish forces arrived in Macorix country, the Indian warriors melted away, vanishing into the forested hills. The Adelantado's troops were unable to pursue them into the heavily wooded mountains. Their armor, long lances, swords and other weapons were suited more for combat in open spaces. In the dense, concealing forests that the Macorix knew so well, the Spaniards were at a disadvantage and withdrew.

Bartolomé, however, continued to be troubled by the threat of Guarionex. Perhaps he also was determined to personally avenge himself on the cacique he had once held and released. So Bartolomé returned with fresh forces and attacked the Macorix anew, waging war for three months, until in the end, he had subdued them and recaptured Guarionex.

Six hundred Macorix were also taken captive. Now Columbus had prisoners of war to send to Spain. Pleased to have valuable slaves to ship home, the Admiral loaded the captives aboard the two ships that sailed for Spain in October 1498. Mayobanex was left behind to die in prison on the island. Guarionex was also imprisoned.

By the time the Macorix were suppressed, the system of

tribute levied upon the Indians in the Vega and Cibao had completely broken down. Many of the caciques who had held the Taino communities together had resisted the gold tax and had been removed or had fled. Their villages had become disorganized and unproductive.

The Adelantado recognized finally the folly of Columbus's policy. The tribute in gold, the blood tax, was a failure. Bartolomé decreed that, henceforth, cotton and cassava would be accepted in place of gold. But it was already too late. So many caciques had been removed and the harassment of the Indians had been so harsh for so long that the fabric of Taino life in the central part of the island had been severely damaged. These once prosperous districts had become zones of famine, disease and despair.

CHAPTER EIGHT

Subjects of the Crown

The end of the tribute, however, did not end the oppression of the Tainos by the Spanish. The failed blood tax was replaced by a new program of exploitation no less inhuman, a brutal system of forced labor.

The hopes for quick wealth that Columbus had inspired in the Spanish had been frustrated. Many colonists blamed Columbus and were critical of him. The ambitious Francisco Roldán, who had plotted earlier against the Adelantado, took advantage of this situation to benefit himself and his followers. He pressed the politically weakened governor to grant certain choice lands to him and to his men.

Columbus's power had so diminished by this time that he felt compelled to give in to these demands. So, in 1499, he granted Roldán and his group tracts in the Vega and Xaraguá, including the right to use the labor of whole communities of Tainos who lived on them. Then, to satisfy the colonists who had remained loyal to him, Columbus gave them similar grants of land together with the use of their caciques and Indians.

The historical rights of the Tainos to their land and to their liberty did not exist in the eyes of the colonists. Such concepts of freedom and human dignity applied only to themselves. The Spanish called the native Indians "dogs," and they had come to regard them as little more than animals. So the unfortunate Tainos were forced to farm, to collect gold and to work for the settlers as servants, if not slaves.

The pretense that the Tainos were not, in fact, slaves was kept up in order to please the Queen. Isabella was still fond of the Tainos and insisted that they be treated kindly. The queen had been angered by the unauthorized trade in slaves that Columbus had taken upon himself to begin. So, in June 1500, she not only ordered that the commerce in Tainos cease but that all owners of slaves in Spain surrender them on penalty of death and return them to Hispaniola from whence they had come.

By now, the sovereigns were weary of defending Columbus from his many critics among the Spanish nobility. The majority of settlers had left Hispaniola disappointed and returned to Spain to join in the chorus of criticism of the Admiral; they complained that his policies as governor had been too heavy-handed and controlling. In the seven years since his return to the island, Columbus's reputation as an administrator had suffered. In that time, he had failed also to deliver on his promises of wealth to the King and Queen.

So in August 1500, two caravels arrived in Santo Domingo with the freed slaves and with Francisco de Bobadilla who had been chosen to replace Columbus and become the new governor. Bobadilla, in fact, arrived as Columbus was putting down a mutiny. Outraged that the Admiral had found it necessary to hang Spaniards, the new governor had Columbus and his two brothers, Bartolomé and Diego, forcibly removed from the island and placed aboard the caravels in chains. In October 1500, Columbus left for Spain, never to govern Hispaniola again.

The fortunes of the Tainos improved little under the rule of Bobadilla. Indians were no longer rounded up and shipped to Spain as slaves, but slavery, by another name, was still their lot. Bobadilla was determined to increase the flow of gold to Spain so he promised the three hundred or so remaining colonists rewards for the precious ore. He granted them special licenses and gave them numbers of Indians to do the work. The settlers changed the Taino method of collecting bits of gold by hand to surface mining. They provided the Indians with metal tools to dig for gold in the rocky stream beds, mainly at San Cristóbal.

The Spanish overseers at the mines cared nothing for the Tainos' well-being. Indians were forced into work gangs and labored long hours in the hot, humid climate. They were poorly fed, carried heavy loads and were so overworked that disease was rampant among them. So many died that constant replacements were required.

Bobadilla's term as Columbus's successor was a brief two years. In that short time, however, he had shown that Hispaniola could yield a significant amount of gold. In April 1502, a great Spanish fleet of thirty vessels entered the prospering harbor of Santo Domingo. The new site for the capital had indeed proved to be a good choice. Santo Domingo had an excellent harbor and the land was well suited for a Spanish town; it was fertile, had sufficient rain and was near the goldfields at San Cristóbal and Cibao. A number of Spaniards had gone to live there with their Taino servants.

The great fleet brought in some twenty-five hundred colonists and supplies and a new governor, Don Nicholas de Ovando.

The Spanish sovereigns prized the gold of Hispaniola, but they also had a duty to spread Christianity there. The King and Queen had directed Ovando to improve relations with the Indians. The Tainos were to be treated kindly and "lovingly taught" the tenets of the Catholic faith to prepare them for conversion. The Queen had specifically forbidden enslavement of the Indians, insisting instead that they be paid wages for their labors. The Tainos were to be considered subjects of the Crown with rights and liberties; they were also to have the responsibilities of subjects, such as paying taxes to the sovereigns on their lands.

The hordes of Spaniards pouring into the island must have dimmed any hopes the Indians still had of dislodging the unwanted colonists. In fact, the great numbers of new arrivals further stressed their already failing farms. Though the Spanish brought provisions with them, these could not sustain the settlers long. Soon the newcomers, too, would depend on the Indians for food.

These Spaniards, like those who preceded them, were mainly opportunists who were intent on making a quick fortune and returning to Spain. They understood little of conditions on the island. The seeds and plants they brought with them were again often unsuited to the local soil and climate. So in a matter of months the shortage of food became more severe.

To make matters worse, the Spanish failed to take the growing cycle of the island's principal crop, manioc, into account. Manioc takes nine to eighteen months to mature. By taking the harvesters away from their fields to dig for gold, the Spanish overseers disrupted the timely planting of succeeding crops. As a result hunger and misery worsened in the central districts. Faith in the power of their zemis was the Tainos' only hope. Perhaps the spirit gods would see their plight and punish their oppressors.

Meanwhile, in Spain, the sovereigns waited for news from Hispaniola. Columbus pressed them in an effort to regain favor. His harsh treatment by Bobadilla may have influenced the Queen to listen and to finally grant his request; she financed a small expedition for him. It was to be his fourth and final voyage of discovery. The Admiral would go to the western Caribbean to claim new lands for the Crown.

At this time the large Spanish fleet in Santo Domingo was preparing to return to Spain. By July, all the gold that the Indians had been forced to mine, including a fortune that had been left behind by Columbus and promised to him by the Queen, was hauled aboard the ships and stored for the journey. By coincidence now, Columbus happened to be passing by Hispaniola and saw the fleet about to leave. Prohibited by the Queen from landing on the island lest his presence disturb Ovando, Columbus sent a boat ashore bearing a message to the governor. In it the Admiral advised that the fleet's departure be delayed because he sensed that a storm was imminent. Ovando, however, had little respect for Columbus. He openly mocked the Admiral and contemptuously dismissed his warning.

So the sailing went forward as planned. Bobadilla and the arrogant Roldán boarded the flagship. Then, as the Tainos watched forlornly, their once proud cacique, Guarionex, was taken in chains from the prison and put aboard. The chief was led to an uncomfortable space below deck. After four miserable years of confinement in jail, he was about to be exiled from his homeland and taken to Spain. What further indignities was he to suffer at the hands of the cruel Spaniards? Perhaps he cried out to Yocahú, his god, to take him and to avenge his tormented people.

The magnificent sight of the great fleet setting out to sea could not have lifted the somber mood of the Tainos. The ships sailed eastward along the southern coast of Hispaniola. But only hours after the fleet's departure, as the vessels turned northward around the eastern end of the island, the winds picked up and the hazy Caribbean sky dimmed with an eerie light. The sea birds disappeared. A rising swell developed and the sky darkened further. The winds grew steadily worse.

Indians living near the shore recognized these signs and fled inland. They must have feared what was about to happen. Then the terrible force of a tropical hurricane slammed into the fleet. Ships were tossed about like toys, smashed and torn apart by the tempest and sunk. The flagship went down, taking Bobadilla, Roldán and Guarionex with it. As if it were cursed, the gold that had been extorted so cruelly from the Tainos, the first big shipment of promised riches from the Indies, was taken from the Spanish and claimed by the sea.

Was the catastrophe an omen? Were the zemis finally showing the Spaniards their anger? Would the strangers heed the warning and go home?

The storm took a terrible toll. Some five hundred lives, mostly crewmen, were lost at sea; almost all thirty ships of the fleet were sunk. Only one vessel made it through the hurricane to reach Spain. As fate would have it, that particular ship carried Columbus's personal fortune in gold. The Admiral, however, had little time to enjoy it. He died in Spain four years later, in 1506, at the age of fifty-five.

The hurricane uprooted trees and flattened Indian villages. It also leveled Santo Domingo, whose buildings were made of thatch and wood. But the storm did little to discourage the newly arrived settlers. Excited still by stories of riches to be found in Hispaniola, they set out eagerly for the gold fields.

Once again the Tainos observed Spaniards, weakened by a long sea journey and unused to working in the Caribbean sun, underestimate the task before them. The newcomers rushed in to begin the heavy work of mining, lacking proper tools and knowledge of what they were doing. Greed motivated them, and it drove them to disaster. In a matter of months, malnutrition and fevers claimed about a thousand of the newly arrived colonists.

The loss of Spanish lives was only one of the many problems facing Governor Ovando. The provisions that had arrived with the influx of new settlers had dwindled, and he could no longer obtain sufficient food from the Indians to feed the colony. The Tainos passively resisted Ovando's efforts to increase productivity. Ovando, who had considerable experience in military administration, wanted to discipline the Tainos, but the Queen's affection for the Indians prevented him from taking the stern measures he preferred.

CHAPTER NINE

"As Free Men"

The Queen's protective attitude toward the Indians created difficulties for Ovando. The colonists depended on the Indians to do most of the labor, but the Tainos were avoiding contact with the Spanish and would not willingly work for them. Wages meant nothing to the Indians. In their culture, people had worked for their families and communities and had managed happily without wages for centuries; they had no concept of money and no experience in being paid for work.

Ovando sent a message to the Queen, complaining that, if left on their own, the Indians would not work for the Spanish. He waited months for her reply. In 1503, he received new directives. The first instructed him to resettle the Indians into villages near the Spanish communities so that the Tainos might better observe and learn Christian ways in preparation for their conversion. The second decreed that the Tainos must cooperate by working in construction, farming, and mining for such wages as the governor deemed appropriate. To achieve these goals, the caciques were to recruit numbers of Indian workers "as free men, however, and not as servants."

The Queen, thousands of miles away in Spain, must have believed that her orders would protect the Indians and see to their fair treatment. But, unwittingly, she had played into Ovando's hands. He used the Queen's directives cleverly to enhance his powers to subjugate the Tainos. Resettlement meant to him that the Indians had no legitimate claim to their ancestral property. So the governor decided to bring all of Hispaniola under Spanish control.

Despite relatively peaceful relations with the Tainos of the southwestern districts, Ovando was determined to assert his rule over them. The great cacique of the area, Behechio, had died, and the territory was now the domain of Queen Anacaona. The governor sent word that he wished to meet with her and the other caciques in the southwest.

In the fall of 1503, Ovando journeyed overland accompanied by three hundred foot soldiers and sixty mounted cavalrymen to Xaraguá. His troops were armed and prepared for war, though the announced purpose of his trip was to improve relations. The visit was to be a friendly, social occasion for the new governor to meet the beloved Queen. Caciques from all the neighboring districts were invited to this ceremonial meeting.

Scores of chiefs of greater and lesser rank gathered by invitation to demonstrate their peaceful and friendly intentions to the governor. Anacaona, ever gracious and hospitable, once again welcomed the Spaniards and saw to their comfort and entertainment. There was no hint of anything sinister.

But at a prearranged moment, as the festivities were taking place, the governor gave a signal and his troops suddenly attacked the unarmed Indians. The Tainos were caught completely by surprise and overwhelmed. Numbers of caciques and Indians were slaughtered outright. The principal chiefs were herded into the royal hut which was then set ablaze, killing about eighty of them. Still other caciques were hanged. Ovando was relentless, thorough and merciless. Eighty-four caciques died in the treacherous massacre, including Anacaona. Shocked and leaderless, the Indians of the southwest were easily subdued by the Spanish forces.

Ovando also extended Spanish control in the southeastern territory by similarly harsh methods. In that same year, 1503, he sent a ship around the eastern end of the island on a mission to the north coast to search for a suitable harbor to develop as a port. There was a small isle off the southeast province of Higüey where Spanish vessels bound for Spain stopped to take on quantities of cassava bread for the long journey. Other boats took cassava bread from the island to Santo Domingo which had been rebuilt after the hurricane with sturdier stone buildings. The bread was to feed the work gangs in the goldfields.

The survey vessel stopped at the island to take on a supply of cassava bread. In the course of loading, however, a barbaric incident took place. A Spaniard, without apparent cause, maliciously set an attack dog upon the local cacique. The chief was severely bitten and suffered such terrible wounds that he died. The Tainos were so shocked by this vicious murder that they wailed and cried out to their zemis at the chief's burial.

Word of the unprovoked killing spread quickly to the Indian communities on nearby Higüey. The brutality so incensed the Tainos that it triggered an uprising. This rebellion came to be known as the "war of Higüey."

The full force and military power of the Spanish were used to crush the insurrection. Scores of Indians were killed in a series of bloody skirmishes. Others were captured, tortured, burned or hanged. Many prisoners became slaves. In 1504, the cacique of Higüey, who had escaped, was captured, taken to Santo Domingo and hanged.

After the battles of Higüey, Hispaniola was all but completely under Spanish control. Ovando had eliminated all the major Taino chiefs. Secure now, the governor affirmed that the takeover of Taino lands and their redistribution to the colonists was legal and that forced labor, even for wages, was lawful, also. The evil that began with Columbus's grant of lands to Roldán became official policy and the program was called "encomienda."

Under encomienda, the governor assigned a local cacique together with his villagers and their conucos to a particular Spaniard who had the right to employ his Indians as he saw fit, to farm, or, more likely, to mine gold. This system promised to enrich the Spanish. Four-fifths of the gold that the Indians produced could be kept by the owners and one-fifth was to be collected by the Crown as tax. The governor distributed Tainos and their properties not only to colonists on the island but also to Spanish nobles and royalty in Spain, creating a new class of absentee owners there.

Ovando enjoyed a powerful role. He was in a position to make men wealthy and to reward his friends. Lands and Tainos were assigned at his discretion. Thirty Indians might go to one Spaniard, while forty, fifty or a hundred or more might go to another of higher status. Ironically, the partition of the land and the resettlement of the native peoples were accomplished in the name of the Queen, whose directives had been intended to bring the Indians closer to the Spanish in order to teach them Christian values.

Queen Isabella died that year, 1504. Her husband, King Ferdinand, became sole sovereign of Spain and he finally approved the granting of lands under the encomienda and made it legal. The King, who had never been as sympathetic toward the Tainos as the Queen, now pressed the colony and its governor for more gold. Ovando had even less reason to be concerned about the well-being of his Indian subjects and forced them to work still harder.

Settlers who had productive gold mines were assigned more Indians. They were even allowed to rent Tainos from other colonists and send them into the mines. Work gangs were recruited, and men and women were herded off like cattle to one mine or another and moved sometimes again and again. No regard was shown for the destruction of Taino families and communities. The Spaniards maintained the illusion that these Indians, pressed into their service, were not slaves because they gave them so-called wages. These were often bits of clothing — in keeping with the late Queen's wish that the Indians wear clothes "like reasonable men."

The separation of families was a severe hardship on the Tainos. With their husbands taken away to the mines for six to eight months a year, the wives had more and more of the heavy farm work to do. Forced to labor even harder, and malnourished, the women could not nurse their babies adequately and the infants often died. Indians in the mines were forced to subsist on cassava bread alone. Their diet lacked the fish and meat that the Tainos had formerly obtained by fishing and hunting, and it was therefore deficient in protein and fat. Malnutrition, hard labor, disease and, perhaps, heartbreak and despair all combined to take a heavy toll among the mine workers.

Hispaniola, once an island paradise, had become a prison for the Tainos. The happy life and freedom they had enjoyed before the arrival of Columbus had changed to a harsh existence of endless toil and early death. The sound of women singing in their villages, the joyous areytos and the entertaining games in the plazas were gone. Now grief and hopelessness prevailed in the dwindling communities.

By the year 1508, only about sixty thousand, of the one million Tainos estimated by experts today to have populated the island when Columbus arrived, remained. At the same time, the number of Spaniards in Hispaniola had increased from three hundred to some eight to ten thousand. The Europeans were settled in fifteen major towns located across the island in the remnants of Taino districts.

The decline of the Taino population concerned the Spanish only because it became increasingly difficult to recruit work gangs for the mines. In order to keep the gold coming from Cibao and San Cristóbal, more Indians were needed. This matter was finally brought to the attention of Ferdinand, and, in 1509, the King granted Ovando permission to take Indians from the Lucayan islands (the Bahamas), the isles to the north which Columbus had first discovered, to labor in the mines of Hispaniola.

CHAPTER TEN

A Life of Misery

Spanish slave-raiders invaded the Lucayan islands, rounding up natives to replace the Indians destroyed by the gold mines of Hispaniola. They designated their passive captives as naborias, the lower class of Taino society, so that the Indians could be put into lifelong service without violating the sovereigns' prohibition against enslavement of the natives. Lucayans who resisted, however, were considered to be prisoners of war and made slaves outright.

The slavers tried to pacify the captives with promises to take them to a legendary paradise in the south where the Indians believed their ancestors dwelled. The Lucayans were taken aboard Spanish ships and packed into crowded holds below deck. The poor Indians could not have imagined the horror of their journey. Jammed unmercifully into dark pens without food, water or sanitation, they began to die at sea within days. An account of this atrocity tells that "a ship might sail without compass or chart, guiding itself solely by the trail of dead Indians who had been thrown from the ships."

Lucayans who survived the trip to reach Hispaniola fared no better. Weak from starvation and unused to the arduous labor of mining, they also succumbed to overwork and disease. But the welfare of the Lucayans did not trouble King Ferdinand; he was concerned only that there be Indians enough to keep up the output of the mines, especially his own, for the King had a number of encomiendas and Indians digging for gold. So the King sent Ovando an order to increase the number of Indians working in the mines and somehow feed them.

Before the end of the year 1509, however, Ovando retired and a new governor took control of the colony. He was Diego Columbus, elder son of the late explorer. Diego had loyally represented his father's constant demands for large profits from his expeditions in the royal court and risen to privilege by marrying the King's niece. The King directed the young Columbus to do more to increase the flow of gold. Though the native population had been greatly depleted, and only some forty thousand Tainos remained on Hispaniola, the King insisted that more Indians be put to work in the mines. In 1510, Ferdinand ordered that no less than a thousand Indians be kept in the mines at all times. When this directive failed to satisfy his desire for gold, the King went still further. In 1511, he instructed the governor to force one-third of the whole, dwindling Indian population into the mines.

The condition of the Tainos by now was so atrocious that eyewitness reports from returning priests and colonists of the inhumanities and brutalities had begun to stir the conscience of the Church in Spain. A group of Dominican friars traveled to Hispaniola to learn firsthand what was happening. What they saw shocked them.

The Dominicans invited the governor, other officials and prominent settlers to attend church one Sunday morning in 1511 in Santo Domingo. The colonists understood that the subject of the day's sermon would be important, but they had no idea what it was. At the appropriate moment in the service, a friar, chosen for his eloquence, took the pulpit to speak.

Fray Antonio de Montesinos reminded the congregation of their holy mission to treat the Indians with kindness and respect in order to prepare them to become Christians. Then he condemned the brutality and cruel exploitation of the Taínos under the encomienda system. He berated the colonists in stern clear terms for betraying their Christian principles and responsibilities. The mistreatment of the Indians must end, he warned, and the settlers must mend their ways.

The colonists listened, stunned. They were shocked by the friar's scathing attack. But their reaction was not what the priest intended. The colonists felt neither shame nor guilt. They were angry. Who was this priest to come and criticize them? How dare he call their ways evil? The Indians, to them, were little more than animals, weak and lazy ones at that. No unimportant priest from Spain was going to tell them how to treat the Indians, or to set them free.

The governor, too, was displeased. He had just sent forces to invade and conquer Cuba. He fully intended to subjugate the Taino population and to impose the encomienda system on that island, too. The priest's scornful attitude toward encomienda angered him.

After church that day, the settlers' leaders met. They complained about Fray Antonio and demanded that he retract his criticisms. Finally, it was agreed that the priest would address them again the following Sunday. All week long the colony braced expectantly for a showdown. Would the priest yield?

But Fray Antonio was, if anything, even more critical and forceful that day. He insisted not only that the colonists must release their Indians from enslavement, but he also threatened them with excommunication from the church if they failed to do so.

The risk of being cast out and denied the holy sacraments of the church was intolerable to the settlers. Fray Antonio was now not only interfering with their livelihood, but the priest was also putting their very souls in jeopardy. Had he overstepped his authority? Besides, if encomienda was abolished and the Indians freed, the colony, the settlers and the coffers of the Crown would suffer.

The controversy reached across the water all the way back to Spain where the King appointed a council of religious and learned men to study the problem. The settlers sent a sympathetic Franciscan priest to argue for them and Fray Antonio returned to fight on behalf of the Indians. So many officials and privileged members of the royal court benefitted from the encomienda system in the Indies that the colonists seemed likely to prevail.

But the Dominican friar was not to be denied. He reported the horrors he had witnessed. He did so with such honesty and passion that the King, the council and even his adversary, the settlers' own representative, were won over. Fray Antonio's plea for compassion in the treatment of the Tainos so stirred the conscience of the council that officials met in Burgos and drafted a body of laws to protect the Indians.

This series of regulations, the Laws of Burgos, as they were called, went into effect in 1512 and 1513. Though this

83

code was the first body of laws put to paper recognizing the civil rights of the Indians, and is important for that reason, it was woefully inadequate by today's standards. Nevertheless, it required the settlers to provide somewhat better living and working conditions and a Christian education for the Indians. Settlers were no longer permitted to call the Tainos "dogs" or similar degrading terms but had to use the Indians' true names. Women more than four months pregnant could not be made to work in the mines, but only to do light housework. Indians were not to be beaten or forced to carry heavy loads. And children below fourteen years could not be forced to work, except at light tasks, such as weeding.

But Hispaniola is a long way from Spain, and the Laws of Burgos were largely disregarded. The wretched condition of the Tainos and their abuse by the colonists persisted. Numbers of Indians continued to flee the encomienda, running off to the mountains and forests to forage and to starve; others preferred to drink the poisonous cassava juice. Some mothers even killed their children to spare them a life of misery. The continuing decline of the Tainos of Hispaniola even accelerated. Now only about twenty thousand Indians were left on the island.

In just twenty years since Christopher Columbus's arrival and the establishment of the first Spanish settlement at Isabela, the native Tainos, who had flourished on the island for centuries, were disappearing. The destruction of these gentle people was not limited to Hispaniola alone. The Lucayan islands had been depopulated. The Indians of Jamaica, Puerto Rico and Cuba were also dying under the oppressive rule of the Spanish. The centuries-old Tainos of the Antilles were caught in the relentless jaws of the encomienda system and were being devoured.

Sadly, the Laws of Burgos actually did little to improve the lot of the Indians. But the courageous efforts of Fray Antonio and the other Dominican monks were not in vain. One colonist had been deeply affected by them, and he was to play an important role in the fortunes of the Tainos.

CHAPTER ELEVEN

Free at Last

In 1502, a young man had come from Spain to manage land
that his father had acquired in Hispaniola. Twenty-eight-
year-old Bartolomé de Las Casas was out to make his fortune
like other gentlemen adventurers in the Indies, and he prospered as a planter. But, in 1510, Las Casas was inspired to
become a priest. Not long afterward, the controversy swirl-
ing around Fray Antonio touched him. A Dominican friar
scolded Las Casas for continuing to own an encomienda and
slaves; priests, at that time, were allowed to own property
like other settlers. Until that moment, Las Casas had always
accepted the prevailing system, and he did not believe that he
had mistreated his Indians.

Las Casas appeared to have put the unpleasant rebuke
behind him. In 1512, he learned that a priest was needed in
Cuba and he went there and acquired a choice, new enco-

mienda. Two years passed and, on the surface, Las Casas's attitudes were unchanged. But, inside, the Dominican's reproach may have gnawed at the priest's conscience.

For in 1514, while Las Casas was preparing a service, the Dominican's preaching seemed to echo in the scriptures he read:

> *He that taketh away his neighbor's living, slayeth him; and he that defraudeth the laborer of his hire is a bloodshedder.*
>
> (Ecclesiasticus: Chapter 34, verse 22)

Las Casas recognized now that the forced labor of the Indians was evil and that the cruel treatment of the Tainos was sinful. He felt compelled to make amends for his own exploitation of the Indians and to become their advocate. He vowed to fight to abolish encomienda. To set an example for others, he gave up his lands, released his Tainos and began to preach reform to his countrymen.

Las Casas was strong-willed and determined. He had taken on an unpopular cause, but that did not daunt him. Nor did he hesitate ever to condemn those who opposed him. The terrible state of the Tainos only quickened his resolve. Time was running out for the Indians. The number surviving on Hispaniola had dwindled to some fourteen thousand; the Tainos on Cuba and the other islands of the Greater Antilles were doomed also unless he could save them.

Las Casas knew that moral persuasion alone would not change the attitude of the settlers. The colonists' self-interest had already prevailed over the efforts of the Dominicans and the Laws of Burgos. New, stronger, more enforceable laws were required to bring about change. So, in 1515, the priest traveled to Spain to seek them, and he gained an audience with the King. The meeting went well; Ferdinand was impressed with the priest's plea. But before they could meet again, Ferdinand died, in January 1516.

The new sovereign was to be the king's grandson, Prince Charles I, but Charles, who was only sixteen, was living abroad in Flanders. So Ferdinand had left the affairs of state in the hands of the able, but aged, Cardinal Ximenez de Cisneros until Charles could come to Spain. Las Casas called upon the eighty-year-old Cardinal and pleaded once more for the Indians. The Regent listened with compassion to the horrors and brutalities the priest revealed to him. When he had heard enough, he decided to summon a group of distinguished men to meet with Las Casas for the purpose of reforming conditions in the Indies. Fray Antonio, who had returned to Spain, was a participant in this council.

The council listened to Las Casas and then directed him to draft new laws to better protect the Indians. The priest's proposals called for the end of the encomienda, freedom for the Indians, their religious education and certain measures to help the colonists with their enterprises that would not exploit the Tainos.

Las Casas's plan was accepted by the Cardinal. Mindful of the many pitfalls in administering regulations in the distant Indies, the Regent decided that priests, not military officers or other officials, should oversee the new laws. He chose the Jeronymite order and had Las Casas select three monks to become joint governors of Hispaniola. Las Casas was appointed "Protector of the Indians" and was given responsibilities to advise the new governors.

The three Jeronymites were not pleased with their unusual assignment but were obedient to the Cardinal. They were directed first to end the encomiendas held by the Crown and certain other absentee landholders. Next, they were to relocate the Tainos into new villages. The reluctant monks, inexperienced in governmental administration, could not have guessed the difficulties they would face in implementing Las Casas's plan.

Word of the new regulations reached Hispaniola even before the Jeronymites arrived. The colonists feared that the reforms would strip them of their laborers. So they pushed the Indians even harder in a last desperate effort to exploit them. Now, virtually all Taino men, women and children were pressed into laboring in the mines or on the farms and worked almost to death.

The monks arrived in Hispaniola at the end of 1516. They quickly carried out their orders to end the encomiendas of the Crown and of other privileged absentee owners. The Tainos bound to these lands were freed. But the Jeronymites faced strong opposition when it came to abolishing the system generally.

The monks were faced with a dilemma. On the one hand, it was apparent that unless the inhuman exploitation of the Indians was promptly ended, the few surviving Tainos would soon perish. On the other hand, the colonists made it very clear that, without the cheap, forced labor of the Indians, their mines and farms would produce no gain and there would be little reason for them to remain. The monks could foresee that without profit the settlers would abandon their enterprises and the colony would disappear.

Was there an answer? Bringing in Indians from other islands was no solution. Of the many thousands of Lucayans brought to Hispaniola, all but a few thousand had already died. The Jeronymites sought advice from the colonists and from authorities. If slaves were essential to the success of the colony, they said, then bring them to the Indies from Africa. Already, in Governor Ovando's time, fifteen years earlier, some few African slaves had been brought to the island from Spain as personal servants. Now the idea grew to import numbers of slaves directly from Africa to take over the labor of the Indians.

By this time, 1518, the Cardinal Regent had died and Charles I reigned. The monks counseled the new sovereign to authorize the importation of Africans to the colonies. The young king took this advice and granted permission for black slaves to be sent to work in the Indies.

Meanwhile, the Jeronymite governors went forward with the plan to resettle the remaining Indians into villages. There were now only about eleven thousand Tainos left on Hispaniola. They were to be relieved of their hard labors and be distributed in groups of three hundred to four hundred into separate communities. Each village was to be given livestock, and plans were made to teach the Tainos the Christian faith.

By January of the following year, 1519, thirty Indian villages had been constructed and were ready to be occupied. But the ill-fortune of the Tainos persisted. Before the Indians could take up a new life in these villages, an epidemic of smallpox had broken out on the island. The disease came in with a shipload of new colonists and it spread quickly, devastating the remaining Tainos. Smallpox claimed up to half the Indian population. It spread throughout the Greater Antilles with deadly effect.

The epidemic wiped out so much of the dwindling Taino population that it caused a severe shortage of workers. The Jeronymite governors, trying to protect the Indians, were now faced with saving the colony from ruin. So they appealed to the young King, urging him to send slaves to the Indies as soon as possible. The Africans began to arrive within months. But, as it turned out, they were put to work not in the mines but on the farms, for, by this time, the meager gold deposits had run out. Agriculture was replacing gold as a source of revenue; sugar cane, brought in by the settlers from the Canary Islands off the northwest coast of Africa, was becoming an increasingly important crop.

The few Indian survivors of the smallpox epidemic were moved into the new villages and were free at last. The encomienda system was finally abolished once and for all. But the efforts of Las Casas, Fray Antonio and the others had come too late to save the Tainos. Not enough Indians remained by this time to revive their community. Like an endangered species pushed beyond the point of no return, the Tainos had been driven too far to be rescued from extinction. By 1548, less then five hundred Tainos of pure blood remained on Hispaniola; the fate of these ancient Amerindian people throughout the Caribbean was similar. Although Mestizo children, the offspring of Spanish and Indian parents, lived on Hispaniola from 1493 onward, the genes of West Indians today are overwhelmingly of African and European origins.

The mineral and agricultural wealth sought by the Spanish conquerors did not exist in the islands. The riches of the West Indies were their people, the Tainos, and they were destroyed. There are no longer Tainos planting manioc, no conucos, no joyous areytos and no proud caciques to greet current visitors. Centuries have passed since the last mothers' songs to their daughters faded in the tropical breeze. The Tainos have been a forgotten people, a bit of history encased in a museum, their story untold.

Today the riches of the Indies are once again their people, a different people, generously welcoming thousands of vacationers from around the world. Tourism is one of the islands' most important industries. Visitors travel to the West Indies for vacations in the sun.

But, here and there, the tourist may find a piece of reddish brown clay, a bit of pottery that hints of a vanished race of long ago. And in caves that hikers occasionally come upon, the gloomy, staring faces of zemi spirits carved into the stone walls bear witness still to the gentle Tainos who welcomed Columbus.

Notes

Page 15. South America. Although numbers of Arawaks migrated from South America to the islands of the Caribbean, others remained. Their descendants still live in parts of Venezuela, Surinam and Guyana today, growing manioc and making traditional cassava bread.

Page 15. Pottery. Archeologists have traced the migrations of the Arawaks by uncovering a trail of their telltale, white-on-red pottery. The broken remains of these pots called "sherds" mark the sites of early Arawak settlements. Bits of charcoal dug up with the sherds are analyzed for their carbon-14 content. Because the rate of decay of this radioactive substance is known, the scientists are able to determine the calendar date when the settlements existed.

Taino/Arawak pottery is particularly informative not only because it can be dated but also because it reveals much about the Indians' life. Sherds are collected, sorted and painstakingly fit together like pieces of jigsaw puzzles to reconstruct plates, cups, bowls, waterpots and griddles. Archeologists can estimate the size of an average Taino family and the population of a community at particular times from the quantity and types of sherds they find. The kinds of utensils and pottery suggest what kind of food the Tainos ate and how it was prepared. Stone graters, wide bowls and many griddle pieces, for example, help to tell us that the main food of the Tainos was cassava bread.

Page 16. The buried trail. Many clues to Amerindian life are hidden in mounds of refuse called "middens." Archeologists often find middens after heavy rains have washed earth away from their surfaces to reveal heaps of discarded seashells, fish skeletons, bits of charcoal and sherds. The scientists remove this material carefully, for beneath it there are often layers of debris left from earlier times.

The Tainos created middens at the edge of their villages and used them as garbage dumps again and again over generations. Each level of refuse, therefore, is like a time capsule, providing much information about the people who left it. Archeologists can reconstruct the history of a village by carefully uncovering and collecting materials from the different layers.

Should you ever come to find ancient artifacts or to discover an archeological site, it is important to preserve them undisturbed and intact so that these buried clues to history can be properly studied for the benefit of all.

Page 16. Saladero. The trail of the white-on-red pottery rose up a steep bank of the great Orinoco river and out onto a flat, grassy plain to the village of Saladero. The trail stopped in this out-of-the-way place, consisting of some nineteen stick and mud huts. Here in the bottom of ancient middens, Irving Rouse and José Cruxent found the pottery of the earliest Arawaks. The scientists used carbon-dating methods to determine the age of the pottery. The pots were made at about 1010 B.C. They were almost three thousand years old. No earlier pottery of this type has been found anywhere else as yet. So Saladero is considered the ancestral home of the Arawaks. The history of the Arawaks must have begun here with the potters of Saladero. These craftspeople and the unique pottery they created at Saladero are, therefore, often called Saladoid.

Page 19. Myth. Another Taino myth about creation held that the sea and its fish were formed when thieves accidentally tipped over a calabash where the bones and spirit of a farmer's dead son were stored. Out of the calabash poured water which kept on flowing until the sea was created and the spirit bones had turned into fish.

Page 19. Island Caribs. To die bravely in battle assured the Carib warrior that he would be comforted in the after-life by Taino slaves. Cannibalism was also part of the Caribs' religion. Caribs made a ritual of eating the limbs of fallen Tainos in the belief that they were protecting themselves from revenge by disabling their enemies' spirits. (The Tainos also practiced cannibalism to some degree.)

Some fifteen hundred descendants of the Island Caribs survive peacefully today on a reservation in the northeastern part of the Caribbean island of Dominica. Though few of them are pure-blooded Caribs, these Indians continue to practice and preserve some of their age-old traditions, skills and handicrafts within a self-governing, tribal community.

The Garifuna, or Black Caribs of Nicaragua, are also of Island Carib descent.

Page 32. Sponsor this expedition. It had taken Columbus more than six years to persuade the Spanish sovereigns to provide funds for the voyage. Earlier, the monarchs of Portugal, France and England had rejected his bids for support.

Page 34. Lucayan hammocks. Our word hammock comes from the native term "hamaca." It was in the Bahamas that the Spaniards saw hammocks for the first time and discovered them to be comfortable and ideal for sleeping in the confined space aboard their ships. Until then, sailors on European vessels slept directly on the hard plank decks. The discovery of Lucayan hammocks by the Spanish, in 1492, was to change the way sailors the world over slept aboard ships.

Page 44. The Holy Faith. Queen Isabella and King Ferdinand were deeply committed to the defense of their Christian faith. They feared the spread of Islam and the growth of Muslim power in the eastern Mediterranean and in North Africa. In January 1492, Spanish armies had defeated the Moors at Granada in southern Spain and driven the last Muslims out from the Spanish homeland. Two months later, at the end of March, the sovereigns had ordered the Jews of Spain expelled. The date of Columbus's departure on his first voyage to the Indies, August 3, 1492, was the deadline given the Jews to leave, to convert to Christianity or to be put to death. The sovereigns were determined that Spain would be a purely Christian nation.

Page 45. Heaps of gold. Columbus had promised great profits to the Spanish Crown in return for its investment in his expeditions; he hoped to provide monies that could be used to raise armies and finance new crusades to wrest Jerusalem and the Holy Land from the Muslims who held them.

Page 55. Bondage. Slavery was not uncommon at that time. Columbus had observed bondage in West Africa where the Portuguese had enslaved black tribespeople and in the Canary Islands where the Spanish had enslaved the native islanders.

Page 76. The treacherous massacre. One account of the barbarity at Xaraguá comes from Diego Méndez. Méndez, captain of one of the ships of Columbus's fourth expedition, was a Spanish gentleman of considerable courage. When Columbus and his crew were forced to beach their vessels and became marooned in Jamaica, Méndez heroically canoed more than 450 miles to Santo Domingo to seek help. Discovering that Ovando was not in the capital, he made his way overland to Xaraguá to find him. There he witnessed the atrocity. Méndez was held some seven months by the calculating Ovando before the governor grudgingly sent a ship to rescue Columbus and his men.

Page 81. "Dead Indians." This description was recorded by Bartolomé de Las Casas, the Spanish priest, who lived in Hispaniola at the time. He is the source of much history about the Indians.

Page 90. Importation of Africans. By 1518, African slaves were being imported directly from West Africa into the Spanish dominions of Hispaniola, Cuba, Jamaica and Puerto Rico to work in the sugar cane plantations that were then developing. In 1697, the French claimed the western third of Hispaniola from the Spanish. But the African slaves there fared little better under the French than the Indians they replaced. Led by a freed slave, Toussaint l'Ouverture, the Africans rebelled against the white planters and fought for and won their freedom. In 1804, this French territory became an independent republic that chose to call itself by the ancient Arawak name, Haiti.

The eastern part of Hispaniola, called Santo Domingo after the city Bartolomé had founded, experienced steady economic decline; its population of Spanish settlers and African slaves eked out a mere subsistence for decades. Then, at the end of the eighteenth century, the slave uprising in the western end swept across the island; the slaves were freed here, too. Control of the eastern two-thirds changed hands several times, but eventually, in 1844, it became the Dominican Republic.

Museums and Exhibits

You may find it interesting to see artifacts of the Taino/Arawak culture. Exhibits are found in a number of locations.

In the **UNITED STATES**:

California Museum of Cultural History, University of California, Los Angeles; Lowie Museum of Anthropology, University of California, Berkeley.

Connecticut Peabody Museum of Natural History, Yale University, New Haven; Yale University Art Gallery, New Haven.

Florida The Florida State Museum, University of Florida, Gainesville.

Massachusetts The Peabody Museum of Archaeology and Ethnology, Harvard University, Cambridge.

New Jersey Museum of Natural History, Princeton University, Princeton.

New York American Museum of Natural History, New York City; National Museum of the American Indian, Smithsonian Institution, New York City; The Metropolitan Museum of Art, New York City.

Pennsylvania University Museum, University of Pennsylvania, Philadelphia; Museo del Indio Antilliano, Philadelphia; Carnegie Museum of Natural History, Pittsburgh.
Rhode Island Museum of Primitive Culture, Peace Dale.
Washington, DC National Museum of Natural History, Smithsonian Institution.

In **GREAT BRITAIN**:

Cambridge University Museum of Archaeology and Ethnology, Cambridge University.
London Museum of Mankind, The Ethnography Department of the British Museum; Horniman Museum and Library.
Oxford Pitt River Museum, University of Oxford.
Salisbury Salisbury and South Wiltshire Museum.

In the **WEST INDIES**:

Antigua Museum of Antigua, St. John's.
Barbados Barbados Museum, Bridgetown.
Cuba Anthropological Museum, Havana University, Havana.
Curaçao Curaçao Museum, Willemstad.
Dominican Republic Museum at La Romana; Museo del Hombre Dominicano.
Grenada St. George's Museum.
Guadeloupe Museum of Edgard Clèrc, Le Moule.
Haiti National Pantheon Museum, Port-au-Prince.
Jamaica Arawak Museum on site of Indian village near Spanish Town.
Martinique Musée Départemental, Fort-de-France.
Montserrat The Montserrat Museum housed in a sugar mill, Plymouth.
Nevis Hamilton Museum, Charlestown.
Puerto Rico Capá ceremonial plaza and museum near Utuado in central plateau; Museo Indígena; Museo de Antropologia, Universidadad de Puerto Rico, Río Piedras.
St. Croix St. Croix Museum, Christiansted.
St. Eustatius St. Eustatius Historical Foundation Museum, Orangestad.
St. Thomas Virgin Islands Museum, Charlotte Amalie.
St. Vincent Archaeological Museum in Botanical Gardens, Northern Kingstown.
Tortola Folk Museum, Road Town.
Trinidad National Museum and Art Gallery, Port of Spain.

Museums and Exhibits

Consult local tourism offices and historical/archeological societies to find Taino/Arawak petroglyphs (the images carved in stone). They can be seen in: Anguilla, Aruba, Bahamas (Crooked Island), Barbuda, Bonaire, Canouan, Cuba, Curaçao, Dominican Republic, Grenada, Guadeloupe, Haiti, Jamaica, Marie-Galante, Martinique, Puerto Rico, St. Croix, St. John, St. Kitts, St. Lucia, St. Martin, St. Vincent and other islands in the Caribbean.

Bibliography

American Museum of Natural History. West Indies Exhibit and Hall of South American Indians. New York.

Bourne, Edward G. *Spain In America*. New York and London: Harper & Bros., 1904.

Coe, Michael, Dean Snow and Elizabeth Benson. *Atlas of Ancient America*. New York and Oxford: Facts on File, 1986.

Craton, Michael. *A History of the Bahamas*. Great Britain: Collins, 1962.

Crosby, Alfred W., Jr. *The Columbian Exchange*. Westport, CT: Greenwood Publishing Company, 1972.

Cruxtent, José M. and Irving Rouse. "Early Man in the West Indies." *Scientific American,* November, 1969, p. 42 +

Fagg, John E. *Cuba, Haiti & The Dominican Republic*. Englewood Cliffs, NJ: Prentice-Hall, Inc., 1965.

Fuson, Robert H., translator. *The Log of Christopher Columbus*. Camden, ME: International Marine Publishing Company, 1987.

Hanke, Lewis. *The First Social Experiments in America*. Gloucester, MA: Peter Smith, 1964.

Harrisse, Henry. *The Discovery of North America*. Amsterdam: N. Israel, 1961.

Joyce, Thomas A. *Central American and West Indian Archaeology*. New York: Hacker Art Books, 1973.

Keen, Benjamin, translator. *The Life of the Admiral, Christopher Columbus by his son, Ferdinand*. New Brunswick, NJ: Rutgers University Press, 1959.

Lovén, Sven. *Origins of the Tainan Culture, West Indies*. Göteberg: AMS Press, 1935.

Lowenstein, S., editor. *Proceedings of the Eighth International Congress for the Study of the Pre-Columbian Cultures of the Lesser Antilles*. Tucson: University of Arizona Press, 1980.

Mac Nutt, Francis A. *Bartholomew de Las Casas*. Cleveland: The Arthur H. Clark Company, 1909.

———, translator. *De Orbe Novo, The Eight Decades of Peter Martyr,* Vol. 1. New York and London: G. P. Putnam's Sons, 1912.

Morison, Samuel E. *Admiral of the Ocean Sea: A Life of Christopher Columbus*. Two vols. Boston: Little, Brown & Company, 1942.

———. *Christopher Columbus, Mariner*. Boston and Toronto: Little, Brown & Company, 1942.

———, translator and editor. *Journals and Other Documents on the Life and Voyages of Christopher Columbus*. New York: The Heritage Press, 1963.

National Museum of the American Indian. West Indies Exhibit. New York.

Olsen, Fred. *On The Trail of the Arawaks*. Norman: University of Oklahoma Press, 1974.

Sanders, Ronald. *Lost Tribes and Promised Lands*. Boston: Little, Brown & Company, 1978.

Sauer, Carl O. *The Early Spanish Main*. Berkeley and Los Angeles: University of California Press, 1966.

Simpson, Lesley B. *The Encomienda in New Spain*. Berkeley and Los Angeles: University of California Press, 1950.

Steward, Julian H., editor. *Handbook of South American Indians,* Vol 4. Washington, DC: United States Government Printing Office, 1948.

Waldman, Carl. *Encyclopedia of Native American Tribes*. New York: Facts on File, 1988.

Williams, Eric. *From Columbus To Castro, The History of the Caribbean 1492–1969*. New York and Evanston: Harper & Row, 1970.

Wilson, Samuel M. "Columbus, My Enemy." *Natural History,* December, 1990, p.44 + .

Bibliography

———. *Hispaniola, Caribbean Chiefdoms in the Age of Columbus.* Tuscaloosa and London: The University of Alabama Press, 1990.

———. "Peopling the Antilles." *Archaeology,* September/October, 1990, p.52+.

Index

Index

ABOUT THE AUTHOR

Francine Jacobs grew up in an oceanside community on Long Island, New York. She loved exploring the beaches and tidal pools in search of seashells, starfish and other treasures of the sea. She now lives in Pleasantville, New York, with her husband, a physician, but she remains an avid beachcomber.

Mrs. Jacobs is the author of twenty books for young readers on a variety of subjects. In 1986 her book *Breakthrough, The True Story of Penicillin,* won The New York Academy of Sciences' Fifteenth Annual Children's Science Book Award.

"The idea for *The Tainos: The People Who Welcomed Columbus* began on the Caribbean island of Anguilla," Mrs. Jacobs says. "One day a young Anguillian friend told me about a cave he had discovered that had strange faces carved on the stone walls. So I made my way there to see the carvings for myself. That was the start of this exciting project."